GOOSE SUMMER

GOOSE SUMMER

STORIES

by
Carol Reese Samson

Owl Canyon Press

First Edition, 2021
All Rights Reserved
Library of Congress Cataloging-in-Publication Data

Samson, Carol Reese
Goose Summer : Stories —1st ed.
p. cm.
ISBN: 978-1-952085-05-5
Library of Congress Control Number: 2020952240

Owl Canyon Press
Boulder, Colorado

For John

CONTENTS

I.

II.

I.

Those life forms best suited to a changing world, the most aggressive and adaptable species, some would say the least poetic, survive: poison ivy, catfish, the mummichog, a topminnow that can live in the dirtiest water imaginable. The quirky ones, the brides of particular habitat, the place-faithful, may find their biological lineage at a dead end . . . . Commonly, they are the first to become extinct. In small numbers, confined to a single patch of landscape, and reliant on a precarious niche, risks escalate.

Ellen Meloy, *An Anthropology of Turquoise*

Experience is . . . a kind of huge spider-web of the finest silken threads suspended in the chamber of consciousness and catching every air-borne particle in its tissue.

Henry James, *The Art of Fiction*

INDEXICAL

This is the terrain. It is a land covered with darkness so that people outside it cannot see anything and they can sometimes hear voices of women and the sound of horses neighing and cocks crowing, and they know that someone lives in there, but they do not know what kind of someone it might be, and, sometimes, when I find the people, they are there, frozen, like in this picture of my Aunt Ruth and me, and I see, again, how dark she was, how tall with thick black hair, her jawline severe, her nose straight as a pencil and, in this picture, you can see I am five years and small and holding a birthday cake, but what you cannot see, in the black and white and dark, is that I have red hair from my father's side and Ruthie is dark and is on my mother's side, my grandmother's sister, but my grandmother is soft, soft, and dimpled, and, if you look closely, you will see Ruthie's hand on my shoulder like she is claiming me, and you will see my plaid dress, red and green, belted in the back, my black shoes with a black strap, my socks folded over at the top and you can see that Aunt Ruthie and I have come outside on the steps in winter, in January, in cold, and we are standing on the top step of the porch of my grandmother's red house and there is snow on the edges of the concrete steps, and I know, if you look closely, you can see the shadow of my grandmother invading the picture from the bottom step and how the winter sun is bright and how my grandmother is bent over her box camera, seeing Ruthie and me in a bubble that moves on the top, adjusting it again and again, trying to find us, to hold still, and what you cannot see is that my grandmother's house had a basement, a dark land with a room where Gary lived, Ruthie's son, a boy with curly black hair who stayed in my grandmother's basement for many years, coming upstairs now and then to bring pictures, paintings he had done of Gyro, the collie dog, of bowls of goldfish, of his own dark face with brown eyes, coming up from the basement when he wanted some homemade bread or oatmeal, and you would never know from this frozen picture space that when I was in first grade, my grandmother always sent Gary to my school to wait for me at the end of the day to walk me home and then he would go back to the basement to live and I myself can only imagine that, after she put Gary in the basement, my Aunt Ruthie with the pencil-straight nose married my Uncle Mac, because that was before I was born and all I remember is that Mac was bald and worked for Kodak and had all sorts of cameras in his house and that he told me about lenses, about color film, about how we are indexical, things captured on the film and held to the paper by chemicals and, then, showed me how a Polaroid camera makes pictures come out in ten seconds and, as I recall, he took pictures of me and Aunt Ruthie, and, afterward, I would stand by his chair and watch the two of us, Ruthie and me, come into being again, all hazy and yellow and resolving, and, truth to tell, I did not trust the Polaroid, even then, because it turned us sulfur color and sallow and, while I was happy to have the picture come so quickly, I knew it was a lie, but, then, even though I felt Polaroids are yellow untruths, even though we are fading in them always and you cannot get the film anymore, I do keep all of these remnants of us, photos and Polaroids, in a box, snapshots of Uncle Gary, grown to a man, dark in his military uniform, and even this one, the last Christmas we were all together where you can see my grandmother's grey dress, my grandfather standing with his cane and you can see the decorations, the way my grand-mother scotch-taped the holiday cards to the back of the front door, and you can see all of the silver tinsel my grandfather put on the tree, placing it a strand at a time, so he could save it for the years to come and I'm behind them, wearing a plaid skirt, white blouse, penny loafers, and there, at the center, our dog, a black dog in black and white, looking at the camera as if he had done this pose many times before and as if he knows we, all of us, are victims of the photograph that cannot mean without us, that waits for us to give it words in black and white, to define the fake cotton snow lining the windows and a skinny tree that does not, in this state of array, know itself, and, of course, this one picture here, this one, the vintage photo card that my grandmother gave to me, an historic photograph of her Ger-man grandmother taken in 1900 at her funeral somewhere in Germany, and printed on cardboard, a dark picture of a thin woman, her hair piled on her head, lying in a dark casket of wood and my grandmother once telling me it was a custom to photograph the dead so that relatives could remember and she told me that, when she was small, she would set the picture up sideways so that her dead grandmother looked like a lady in a ticket booth selling tickets at a movie theatre and she would pretend to buy the tickets from her, her dead grandmother, and I think about that when I look at these, the slides from my grandfather's stereo vision camera, the ones you can only see through his special stereo viewer where you have to insert them and, then, Click—here is my grandmother and Ruthie watching out the window to see Lyda who lived across the street, looking for a car to arrive at Lyda's, for a man to go into the house, a wobbling man, and then, Click—here is my grandmother with her friend Herta, whose hair is a sort of yellow that Polaroids make everybody's hair and who, as a young bride in Latvia, during the war, was forced to watch her husband be hanged by Nazi invaders, and, Click—my grandmother with Martha, the Card Lady, who sold cards door to door, a bantam hen of a woman with a hemp bang, knocking door to door, selling greetings, and, then, of course, I have no pictures of the day, her breasts gone bad, my grandmother lay dying, or the moment when Gary's body began to stiffen, his spine and fingers turning to stone, or what happened to Ruthie when, her straight nose pointed at the ceiling, she willingly began to let go of pieces of her, and, you could not guess this from this picture of the birthday cake, but I would go to the hospital where Ruthie lived to sit with her and to listen even when all she said was "Who?" and "Who?' when I told her anything, and I would bring her to my house for dinner, show her the Polaroids, touch her hand and Ruthie, the straight and unadorned Ruthie, her movements like a puppet doll, her hand making fork trails in the mashed potatoes, would sing her incantation, "Who?" and "Who?" and "Who?" and, also, what you cannot know, is how I move to the land in darkness and stand outside, listening to the women whispering and to the roosters crowing, to the murmurs in the red house in January, in black and white, and how I find them, these dark things, their hands on my shoulder, their bodies near me as we stand on the porch, indexical, as we wait for the chemicals to affix us or as we wait for someone to set us upright as if we were in a ticket booth, and all the time knowing, as I do, as a poet said, that we are bound to all that is lost, to all that will leave no trace.

RHINO

1.

It must have been the stone lions, rough-hewn, at the entrance to the park. I was walking there, in the town park where, a hundred years ago, a town banker had placed two monuments, the lions, side by side. There were yellow leaves falling. The Farmer's Market was holding its last Saturday market. A guitar player played music about endings and farmers were selling radishes and golden beets and one grey-haired woman sat next to a bucket of yellow sunflowers and the bee lady sold honey from bees that live in high mountains over 10,000 feet, bees that would be gathered and transported to the almond groves of California for the winter. I passed by the crocheted-hats-and-afghan lady and the masseuse and used book man and the woman who lived in a trailer by the river and stitched cloth napkins with moose patterns.

It might have been the stone lions' eyes, small drilled holes, their blind-eyed stare, because I turned there to go down the last row of white market tents and saw the booth, a card table with a wire pen. A bearded man sat under a sign that said: "RHINOS FOR SALE/$50.00." The man had an earring in his ear, a turquoise chip, and he had one rhino, not too big, in the pen. The rhino stood on some straw staring out at something. There was a dog bowl at its feet. It did not move. It was a stoic thing amidst the children and the dogs and the straggling couples and the Amish man selling pies.

I asked the man, Would this rhino be hard to raise?

He said, No, you just have to know it has no teeth in the front. To eat, it has to reach with it lips. It folds food in its front lip.

I asked, Have you raised many?

He said, I used to raise camels, sell the camel milk. Rhinos are more passive. Just keep it in the backyard.

I asked, Do they get angry?
He said, Only when the wind blows.

2.

When I was a child, my Father told me a rhinoceros lived in the backyard, and pointing toward the window, he would say, Look out there. Do you see a white one or a black? Or is it a blue one with black markings?

I knew he always wanted to own a rhino of his own. Once he called the Big Animal Rescue people and asked if there might be a rhino available. I could hear him answering their questions: did he have a veterinarian who could vouch that he vaccinated his animals? Did he have a fenced yard? Were there other animals in the house? Did he have a soft bed for it or would it sleep on the couch? Would he walk it? Did he have references?

As I sat by him on his reading chair, he showed me old drawings of a rhinoceros painted on the cave walls of Chauvet, of horses running with buffalo, and of the places where shamans traced their hands in red-powder, making spots on the walls, framing the palm and fingers of a single hand, creating a red totem to tame the beasts. Father said I should read Pliny, the Elder, and he reached for that book. And once, his voice ever so serious, Father told the story about the King Manuel of Portugal who, in the summer of 1515, wanted to show his rhino to the Pope. The rhino had come to Lisbon in a wooden ship, and the King housed it near the palace. Father said the King brought it to a stadium to fight an elephant. Surely, everyone thought, the rhino with its fighting horn would win against a lumbering elephant. Father said that the King stood the beasts together and that some-one had draped the rhino's head and back in orange and yellow cloth with bangles. But the crowd in Lisbon cheered, and, said Father, the noise fright-ened the elephant and it ran from the arena and out into the hills. What is important here, my Father told me, leaning close, is that someone took time to draw the beast, its horn, the texture of the folds of skin. Someone trans-lated it, is how my Father said it.

My Father's voice waffled. This, I knew, was the sad part. When the King of Portugal prepared to send the animal to the Pope, Father went on, the sailors secured the animal, strapping it in the wooden boat, using chains to keep it still. Some say, Father said, the ship sailed off toward Rome and dark clouds came up and the boat rocked and turned and tilted in the wind and all things were tossed into the sea. Except the rhino. It was tied there, strapped in by chains, unable to break the bonds, unable to swim. My Father's eyes filled with water as he described the taunting of the seagulls and the boom-ing of the thunder and the flapping of the sails. The rhino must have heard the tearing of the ship's wooden timbers and its own bellowing, its grunting calls, in the howling of the winds as all went down to the bottom of the sea.

3.

I think often of my childhood pets and of captivity: the small turtle, with its red painted shell marked with the name of a movie cowboy, that was pur-chased at the dimestore, the Easter chicks who lived in a box in the kitchen and created gruelly masses of green poop, the guinea pig and her son who sang staccato chirping sounds and mated with each other and had a child so Father changed the male's name from Jock to Oedipus, the salamander with its palm-tree fringe of skin around its face who fed on live crickets, the goldfish tribes, found floating upside down in the fishbowl then flushed down the toilet, the blue parakeets that flew out of the house to somewhere, the frog from the Frog Rodeo that hopped under the couch and was eaten by the dog, the starling bird named Francis that we found fallen from a nest and the Bird Lady who lived next door who said, We'll see, we'll see, because, you know, you cannot save them all.

4.

My Father's stories became my dreams. I would consider the rhinoceros in its orange and yellow drapery looking at me with its sad eye. Sometimes in the daylight I tried to draw the rhino, at first in shaman drawings in red crayon and then with the colored pencils Father gave me, creating them in purple and green and pink. I came to paint with oil paint and made the rhi-nos look like those in science books. I made surreal ones with many heads. Once I painted out a wooden boat with window holes, each window with a rhino looking out. I filled the walls of my room with drawings. I detailed the rough coat, the kind of goiter chin. I rescued them in images.

Then I looked at Durer's drawings in my Father's books. Durer never saw a rhino, my Father told me, but his beast seemed worldly wise. When I looked at it, Durer's version seemed to have its own Thunder Jacket, the kind Father put on our dog when the dog heard strange noises and began to shake. I could see that the rhino's sides seemed to be etched with underwater plants and strewn with seaweed blossoms. Its hindquarters looked costumed as if it wore frilly and pleated pants and, up under its neck, I saw it had a kind of bib, a flattened plate near its jowls, a solid piece of armor. Mostly, I favored its eye. The creature seemed resigned to its fate, willing to be defined by someone who did not know it.

5.

Perhaps, then, it was the stone lions in the park. There were yellow leaves falling. I bought the rhino. It is in the backyard tethered to the tree. I made a fenced pen. I bought a Walmart child's pool which I fill with water each day. I go out every morning to feed it grain. Sometimes I hold the grain out in my hand and feel it work its lips across my palm because it has no teeth in the front. Sometimes I just sit with it. I suspect it is waiting for me to tell it stories of that King in Portugal or of Durer. I may do that in time. But, for now, I cannot because sometimes, when I look into its glassy eyes, I suspect it is aware that I will someday translate it or will frame it in images so limiting that it cannot get out. I think it knows it is peculiar, an oddment in this world. Peculiar things know. And sometimes when I see its eyes fill with water as it stands in my backyard next to a blue plastic pool, I know it is listening to something I cannot hear, some ancient and internal bellowing coming to it on the wind.

GOOSE SUMMER

Goose summer. Goose summer. Goose summer. Goose summer. Goose summer.

She said it as she walked.

Goose summer. Goose summer. Goose summer.

Head down, watching the cracks in the sidewalk.

Goose summer. Goose summer.

One day I realized she was saying, "Gossamer."

*

Martha, the Card Lady, came to my grandmother's house selling boxes of cards from a hemp bag slung over her shoulder. She was a friend of my grandmother's, a thin woman with a fluff of hair over her scalp and cheekbones covered in onion paper stretches of flesh. She sat at the table and made fan-shaped passages of cards. Kittens with butterflies. Storks bearing babies held in blankets in the sky. Brides and grooms leaving the church in a blossom of rice. Martha had one card for each celebration. Buy twelve, get all the rituals of human life for $1.50.

My grandmother gave her toast and butter as we sat at the table, drinking coffee flooded in milk. My sister and I watched Martha. She consumed the toast in pecks, like a small bird, her fingers turning in on themselves, the dark of her eyes moving back and forth even when she sorted cards. We saw her old dress had been washed many times, the cotton fraying at the button holes, the side-ears of beltloops missing the belt.

My grandmother bought cards every time Martha came to the door. She kept them in the coat closet, twenty or thirty boxes, like Chinese promises.

*

I read in an old book that there existed once a Solitary Bird with a long neck. In the detail on the parchment map, this ancient Solitary hides in spotted trees with tufted branches. Tall and thick, with feathered neck and crown, it is an odd and quiet thing. It sends up no alarum, no chirp. It waits and watches. It stands and turns its head, looking with one orange eye. Its chest is a frontlet of black velvet.

And the Solitary Bird struts and preens itself and keeps very clean. Its toes are hard scales. It can run with quickness in the rocks. It does not fly at all, but it can flap its wings. It is a bird of the woods. It feeds on figs.

When it is caught, it sheds tears.

*

Martha brought the dress out, holding it like a sacrament cloth draped over her wrists.

My grandmother had taken us to Martha's house, a basement apartment in a bungalow down the street. It was a dark space, bluish light and dust motes and a Jesus calendar on the wall. Martha gave us thin tomato soup made with water, not milk. She gave us red and white peppermint candies for dessert. The candy was sweet in my mouth. I held it under my tongue. My grandmother spoke of President Eisenhower and asked, Did Martha know his wife lived in Denver?

Martha listened, her eyes darting. Sometimes she licked her finger and dotted up imaginary bits of cracker crumbs. She nodded in the wrong places. She made a sort of whining sound.

Jesus watched us eat our soup.

We sucked the peppermints, aware that the blinds on the windows were drawn, that the room smelled of old newspapers, that the table had no cloth. Our grandmother was talking about green stamps, about saving for a waffle maker, when Martha got up and went to the bedroom and brought out the dress.

*

I know a poem about Saint Kevin who knelt in his cell stretching his upturned hand out of the window. His cell was narrow, his arm stiff.

A blackbird landed on his hand. It settled down and nested. And Kevin held his hand like a branch in the sun and the rain, feeling the warmth of the eggs and knowing the flight of the young. He saw the way the light made the blackbird blue. His eyes weary, arm numb, he knew the agitation when the large bird kept the nest, fended off the squirrels. As the underearth crept through him, he waited until the small birds learned and lifted and became a gauzy shift against the sky, aswim. Then he listened for their voices across a great space.

*

My grandmother buried the dogs and cats in the backyard under the pine tree. She had planted a row of hollyhocks there near the fence and in summer it looked like a row of dancers with plumed skirts, pink and white, and one year deep purple. On our birthdays she made us stand by her roses, next to the pine tree, holding our cakes. She had a black box camera. She looked at us through a circle bubble in the top that turned us upside down.

In later years I would try to remember the color of my third-grade dress or of the hollyhocks that year, but everything was in black and white. And then it didn't matter. What I liked to look at most was the way my grandmother's shadow crept across the lawn and rose in front of us like revelation.

*

The dress was a child's dress, small pink stripes smocked in tidy rows and a broad white collar, homemade. The dress was stiff and smelled of earth. It was soiled, dirtied with something.
Martha leaned over the table.

How old are you, child?

Seven, I said.

And your sister?

Five.

Martha spread the dress over her chest and patted it. She made a sound I had never heard before, a rupture of syllables like a bible woman standing on a seashore.

My grandmother rose from the table. She moved behind Martha, put her hand on Martha's shoulder, and took the dress. Martha clutched her bosom like the dress was still there. She was moaning.

Martha, stop now. My grandmother said.

But Martha could not stop. She rocked back and forth, her eyes darting to the ceiling.

Is this your child's dress?

Yes.

You've kept it in the drawer?

Yes.

How long, Martha?

Martha's mouth was puckered like a gathering thread. She rocked on her heels, head back now, studying the dark.

1929.

Did she die then, Martha?

On a swing. On a swing.

In the park across the street?

Rising to the sky. Rising to the sky.

And she slipped out?

Hit her. Hit her. Cracked her.

The swing, Martha?

I was pushing.

And Martha was a bantam hen, moving in circles, making a throaty sound, looking at the ground. My grandmother led her to the table and put her in a chair. She folded the dress and put it back in the bedroom. She heated water and, taking tea bags from her purse, made tea in Martha's broken cup, sweetening it with thick honey. She held the cup to Martha's mouth, forced the liquid to her lips.

The steam reddened Martha's face for a moment. In the coffin light of the room, I could see boxes and boxes of cards stacked against the wall.

Jesus watched us with yellow eyes from the calendar.

*

I heard of an old lady in Paris long ago who sat in the arcades in a shop with pale wallpaper. They say she read all day, that she collected teeth of gold or wax or broken bits. A friend told me of a woman who keeps a ball of string and twine and threads of blue embroidery floss that makes it look like a speckled egg. I know a woman who collects marbles. She has one large, glass marble that four glassblowers made together, a globe of the world with continents in orange and green. She said that one of the four died and there will never be a glass marble like that again. Once I found a photograph album in a store far up in the mountains. There were no photographs, only people cut from magazines, well-dressed men in 1930s tuxedos and ladies in red evening gowns, their hair slick velvet, sitting on sofas drinking champagne, and on the pages that followed drawings of babies cut from Gerber ads in magazines, round-faced infants with wide eyes, a curl of hair spinning from each of their heads.

I saw it. It's there where absence is taken back from silence, where love makes its assault on nothingness.

*

That autumn my sister and I played jacks on our grandmother's porch. As the wind pulled the leaves off the trees, we would see Martha, the Card Lady, in her thin coat, a black hat pulled over her head, lugging the bag of cards door to door, moving to the houses across the street. I saw the way her nylons were rolled at her calves at the hem of her skirt and held with rubber bands. I could see the way her body bent.

I looked down at our game, collecting jacks, my hand a brief sweep, quick and sparrow-like and away, claiming the jacks like metal blossoms, like colored stones, a brown one and two blue ones, like toast crumbs. Quiet. Quiet. A breeze brushing through the tree with the orange berries. Yellow leaf drift, wind sort. I hunched my shoulders, bent over the game, spinning threads, webbings across my eyes, filling my ears with wool to stop the sounds of plucking. Gather blossoms, little girl. Gather beads. Sit quiet on the step. Three and four stones now. Sweep of hand. Gather. Quiet. Stone. Hand sweeping in across the cement-cold landing. Put aside the morning. Gather. Shun the accidental bird come from somewhere, white and black with yellow eyes, parading on the branch of the dying tree. Quick and sparrow-like and away, all ten stones, yellow and orange and red and blue, and there by the tree in the wind, say silent words for those who know the winnowing.

THE GRAMMAR OF ORNAMENT

Lines produce lines growing out one from the other. We know that now. The town is so plain, so nondescript. We only put a statue on the courthouse lawn ten years ago. It was the town benefactor and his mother, standing side by side in bronze. Somehow he left here and became a millionaire. He gave us the hospital. So if you stand on the courthouse lawn, you can see our sense of simple line. The buildings date from the 1880s, the hotel the oldest. We painted it pink because someone said it was pink when Teddy Roosevelt stayed in it. We painted the balcony rail, the iron fancy one, white. That's where he stood when he came to hunt bear. That's our main ornament. The rest of the town is just ordinary yellow brick, but we like the plainness. That's why we stay. Some children never leave this town. They choose to spend their lives dropping stones in the White River that runs down to the sea.

Twila, at the Shooting Star Café next to the Bloom shop, she never left. Each morning she made the breakfast rolls, the sausages in white buns that look like deadmen's fingers. She handled the counter as her mother cooked. A stranger could see they were mother and daughter, square jaws, square forehead, a fringe of bangs. Only Twila was the bigger one, a big-boned girl, a salt-of-the-earth girl, who wore a blue cotton dress with yellow flowers that blended in with the wallpaper. She spent her day loading the milk-juice-water cooler behind the cash register, bending, lifting, bending, a flower garden rising over the counter when she stood up, taking your money in her big-palmed hands and giving you a dimpled smile, her eyes like raisins pressed in dough.

Twila grew up opening white bags and stuffing in hamburgers wrapped in wax paper held together with a toothpick, sticking in a bag of chips, marking COKE or 7-UP on the bag, learning letters by spelling kids' names, Basque sheepherder kids, English settler kids, Ute and Hispanic kids' names.

It was her mother Enid's idea to sell hamburger lunches to the high school kids between 11:15 and 11:45 each weekday morning. Twila grew up eating her own sack lunch with the penciled-on letters, sitting behind the counter when the high school crowd came in, her body thickening with time like her mother's. We all knew her, knew her penmanship on the white sacks, knew the loneliness of her eyes watching us eat potato chips at the round table in the back. She was an ornament, part of the architecture of a café with Indian plates hung on one wall and Cowboy plates on the other, and a big shooting star with a yellow tail painted on the window. We knew she would never marry, though she knew every man in town by name. At 5 a.m. the road crew men with orange vests sat at the round table and ate biscuits and gravy, at 6 a.m. the plumbers and handymen sat and talked of back hoes, at 7 a.m. the high school boys bought bags of doughnut holes, tossing them in the air and catching them in their mouths, by 8 a.m. the hospital workers just off the night shift arrived, and by 9 a.m. the artists who had small studios over the general store described their projects. Twila knew them all. She fed them pancakes with berries or gravy biscuits or doughnuts that tasted like cloud.

The Shooting Star Café is only one block from Highway 13. Inside you can hear the larger trucks whiz by carrying cargo meant for Rangley or Craig or Rifle. It's a good sound, one of purpose and pattern. Sometimes Twila liked to stand and look down toward the road. She could feel the glass shake when the large trucks went by. She watched the local farmers, border collies or hay or workers filling up the backs of their pick-up trucks. And from the window she could see Cemetery Hill and the sprinkling of Angus cows that grazed there. She was too far away to hear the river, but she could imagine it as a river full of Time going somewhere she had no need to be.

First thing is, she looked like her mother, but they were not the same. We knew Enid like we knew our left hand. She would slice a penny in half to stretch her budget. She counted eggs in omelettes, leaving egg batter in the bowl, trying to make two and a half eggs appear like three, cutting back to three spots of ham squares and one Kraft cheese slice in the Denver Omelette, six mushroom pieces in the Combo. She made three bread loaves out of the makings for two, the morning toast shrinking before our very eyes. Enid was a worrier. She had to make things measure. And we watched her take control of Twila, correcting the way she loaded the cinnamon rolls into the glass case, telling her to leave the catsup bottles half full, checking the change drawer like a hawk at the end of the day. Ed, her father, just sat in the corner near the refrigerated cooler, head down, adding numbers and licking the end of his chewed pencil and going out to buy more corned beef when Enid told him to.

What we remember when we speak of Twila is not family love. It is an old memory, high school memory of twenty-nine years gone. What we remember is the boy named Roy, tall and freckled, green-eyed. He was the son of a family who had moved in from Steamboat Springs where we knew the hippies were having their way with the town. He was new to us, and we listened to his stories. He was our novelty. He said that his father came here to work at the strip mines, that his father liked the lilacs on the main road as they drove through town, that he stopped his car and said he would raise his family here where there were lilacs right on the road. Roy was young in Steamboat, and he said it was a different place. Sitting in the Café, eating his hamburger taken out of the paper bag marked, ROY, he told us Steamboat stories about hippie bathing pools. Roy was kind. His family came from Nebraska. His mother was named Joy, and his father liked the lilacs, and his two sisters were beautiful. The older one's face appears in the paper in Real Estate ads in town, and the younger one was a cheerleader, a dark-haired girl with yellow streaks in her hair. They all had green eyes. And Roy, he just sat at the round table in the Café and made us laugh from 11:15 to 11:45 when we had to go back to school. Sometimes he stopped at home and brought his guitar. He would sing us a song about a rocket man who went to Jupiter or Mercury, to Venus or to Mars. And in the song, the rocket man's wife and his boy watched the stars and wondered if a falling star was a ship becoming ashes with a rocket man inside.

We memorized everything Roy told us. He was that special. He was something unexpected in our lives.

Twila listened. We know she did. But Twila was one of those people who can disappear, who prefer that you not notice them. Sometimes we thought that she might just blend into the blue flowered wallpaper or that she sat on her wooden stool so you couldn't see her body behind the glass where the chocolate glazed and cinnamon twist rolls were luminous in the artificial light. But the thing is, Roy, he noticed everything. We said Roy just looked into people. He'd sit in the Café at lunch and start to sing his song about the rocket man who chose the stars. He could make his voice do the parts so that we could hear the mother and the boy watching the stars for the rocket man, for the father who preferred traveling into space over staying home.

My mother and I never went out

unless the sky was cloudy or the sun was blotted out.

Or to escape the pain,

we only went out when it rained.

At the corner of the room, Twila would fill the cooler, moving the orange juice and the tomato juice cans onto the metal shelves ever so quietly when Roy was singing, listening to every syllable with her back.

My father was a rocket man.

He loved the world beyond the world,

the sky beyond the sky.

We'd eat burgers and wad up the sacks. Roy was the one who would call out to her as he left to go back to high school. "See ya tomorrow, Twila." Twila was four years older, finished with school, but we knew she watched us at the window or, rather, she watched him go with us down 6th Street to cut across the courthouse lawn. Then she would turn and collect the white sacks. Enid thought they should come up with a way of reusing the sacks. Ed said that would not be sanitary. Twila collected them off the tables each day, patted them flat, and threw them away.

When her mother died, Twila was still young, and we knew she'd keep the business. We took our children in for sausage rolls and orange juice, and we looked at her face, pale and powdery, and noticed that her hair had begun to thin on top, the center part in her hair making a wide road. Enid used to wear those hairnets to cover everything but the bangs. Twila cut her hair short and allowed it, as if she did not ever use a mirror, to begin to reveal her skull. She was fair skinned, a big-boned girl. She did not like the sun, but she did not wear a hat. We could see her balding head as she walked fast to the grocery for supplies or early on a weekend morning in the neon light as she straightened things inside the Café, arriving at 4 a.m. to take over from her father who had baked all night. As long as we knew them, they never took a vacation.

In those days of high school, though, no one took vacations. We made do with fishing or with taking an old canoe down the river or with watching Roy with his dog. Roy had a blue healer hound, a spotty dog with yellow eyes, who waited all day by the bike racks outside the door of the school. And at the end of the day Roy would take him over to the courthouse lawn where the statues are now, and he would toss the frisbee high in the air and that dog would leap against gravity to catch the disc, rising like some feathery thing, running in circles waiting for Roy to toss it again. They were always together, riding in the back of a friend's truck, the dog leaning out the side watching forward as the wind made its ears pull back, or just traipsing down by the river where there were slow pools for fly-fishing and long-bladed grass beds where we could rest in the sun. Sometimes we sat by the river, and he sang to it, his voice asking it to sing him a song, to take him along. The sky was summer blue and the air was fresh and there was Roy, singing to that river that runs down to the sea.

It is odd what we choose to remember, some things coming up in us like a shock of lilacs standing on the side of the road. We cannot stop them. Twila at her window. We can still see that. She changed the name of the Café to the Shooting Star shortly after her father died. We understood. We all said we knew why, but then we forgot about it. We might remember for an instant when we would bring our children in, buying bags of doughnut holes by the dozen, noting that Twila never changed the prices in all that time. It was Twila's handprinted signs on yellow paper that we got used to, her red ink notations: Hamburgers $1.25. And we just stopped talking about it. But the blue boughs come back each time we watch Twila, her hair just embroidery floss, come out of the café at 11:15 and make her pilgrimage across the courthouse lawn, carrying a white sack.

Some children never leave home, we say, nodding to each other. Some children never go out unless the sky is cloudy or the sun is blotted out. Twila never went out anywhere. She buried both her parents on our Cemetery Hill which she could see from the window, and she just kept feeding us. We watched her face, the way she lowered her eyes to us. We ordered birthday cakes from her and croissant rolls for Thanksgiving. We sat in the corner at the round table and told jokes we knew and had forgotten and remembered again and forgot. Thing about a small town is that you can't know yourself and you can't remember everything. You become an ornament. You become what the people say you are. So we watched each other and watched Twila standing at the window, looking at the sky.

We knew she loved him, loved the boy with the green eyes and the song about the rocket man. He was her blue lilac, and yet all she did was hand him his lunch sack each weekday and hope beyond hope that he came in on Saturday for doughnut holes. He was the thing that made her know desire, made her consider, if only for a minute, leaving this town if she could go

28

with him. And she never said a thing. Sometimes the dog who jumped at the frisbee like a bird would sit, head cocked, ears alert, looking in the café where Roy sat talking to us in the morning. Sometimes she'd serve Roy sausage rolls as he sat with the girl he was asking to the prom. It didn't matter. There are things we love because they *are*. People who *are*. We go to find the people who *are*. Twila fed us, and she herself grew bigger and bigger into dresses that zippered up the front. Twila filled herself, and we watched her fingers become sausage rolls, doughy, like her mother's. That was what we saw mostly, that thickening. That was all we could see. That was what she was, we thought.

Some of us will tell you it was a yellow twilight that summer night, the night we saw better. Some will say that you could smell spring in the river. Some of us remember that little red and purple flowers were coming up in the park, the pine trees had found some strength of purpose after the winter and that we could feel it. That night we decided to drive to Rangely to the pre-graduation dance. One of us had a truck, said we should all go together, and Roy said that he would ride in the back with his dog. He said he liked watching time go backward. He said the dog liked the air moving through its fur. It isn't far to Rangely, he said. He would not be cold. And we went, and we danced, and we laughed with the Rangley High senior class, with the friends from the next town that we might come to love someday. We celebrated the fact that change was coming into our lives, that some of us might be leaving, and we started home.

Sometimes, to this day, we search our minds. We try to see a cause—the small marmot or the fawn or even the elk that might have been coming across the road to the water, to the river that was full and loud. But we see nothing. We can only agree on the black space and night and stars, and sometimes, even now, we feel the truck swerve and fishtail in a long, slow arc. We grab the door handles and brace our hold on the windshield. We feel the spinning and the slide and the shift off the road and the turning and tumbling and sudden shaking, the stop, and we are pressed together in the cab and we do not move.

Then the one on top lifts himself up, and pulling himself by the steering wheel, making it out through the window and reaching back to find the hand of the next one and the next. Someone complains of a deep pain in the side. Another has a welt on his head. One holds his arm and moans. We stand. We bend over, breathing toward the ground, and everything is still except for the river. So much darkness and one small moon, no cars passing, the truck stopped from going into the river by a single rock, a chunk of ancient granite that must have rolled from the mountain long ago, loosened by rains. A black night, a cold sky with a few stars and no sound but the hush of water.

Then one of us says, "Roy."

There is no sound, no call. In the darkness, we find the dog thirty feet from the truck, on its side, its tongue pulling from its mouth, its legs twisted, almost going the other way, a broken thing. One of us takes off his shirt and wraps the dog so we can find it if a car stops to take us home. We call out. We stumble on rocks, working our way to the river. Roy is there. We find him at the river's edge. In the gray light from the moon on water, we can see his eyes are open, staring. He has been thrown that far, a hundred feet or so, his body flying and his weight pulling him to the ground, his right hand pointing off, his head looking up at us. One of us bends down. Roy is breathing, but his body is rag-doll loose. And as we look, we see all ruined, see something has happened to his spine. And one of us starts running, running for help, arms flinging wide, running toward Rangely, hoping that a car or a truck will come out of the dark, some chance night traveler. It is cold. We kneel by Roy and tell him that things will be all right. Someone is crying, choking on his sobs. Someone else is whispering to him. Some of us heard someone singing, others say it was just the river.

There are people in town, including his cousins from Steamboat, who will tell you it would have been better if Roy had died, and there is a logic to that. You can learn it from the animals. Most of them take the life of a small thing that cannot live. Swans attack the cygnets. Male dogs, puppies that cry in pain. Elks fight battles for mates. Nature likes strong things. It doesn't nurture the weak. Some people just said he would never be Roy again. Frozen from the neck down, he would age without knowing time. He would gurgle instead of sing. He would not focus on the morning sun or remember the rain. Some people said it was such a shame that it happened on the road with the lilac boughs.

We buried Roy's dog while the doctors worked. We went to his backyard and shoveled up the dirt, the sun just coming up, and then we went back to the hospital, our parents sitting with us and waiting in the hallway. We took breaks, roaming into town, having coffee at Twila's. That's when she heard about it for the first time. We were still wearing the torn clothes, bandages on our foreheads; but there was no pain. We just sat at the round table and tried to understand what came at us. She gave us omelettes filled with cheese. She hovered and listened. She looked over us at the wall. She did not move to the window. She did not look out at the river or the stars. She did not cry.

What she did was go to the grill and put a hamburger on to cook. She found a white sack and took out her father's chewed pencil and wrote ROY on the front. She refilled our coffee, handed us plates of sausage rolls. And when the hamburger was done, she slipped out of her blue apron, Enid's apron, put the burger in waxed paper, added chips, and started out the door. All we could see was her expanse of back as she moved with uneven steps across the courthouse lawn, carrying that white sack like it was worth something.

We sat there, listening to the cooler with the milk and the orange juice making things cold. We did not speak. We just knew we would not be leaving. For the rest of our lives we would be at this table. We would be ornaments, lines growing out one from the other. And we knew that Twila would watch over Roy and that he would never in his life get to eat those burgers that she cooks each day at 11:15 a.m. He would never know who has been sitting beside him every day for the last twenty-nine years, holding his hand as his head moves from side to side and his eyes wander the room, speaking to him in quiet words about the worlds beyond the world, describing a blue healer hound flying like a bird toward a yellow disc, rising like a rocket in the sky.

On weekday mornings as the sun is coming up, we meet at the Café. We sit at the round table at the back. We speak of wheat and weather. We look at the Cowboy and Indian plates on the wall. We study the cosmic windings of the cinnamon rolls in the counter display. The trucks go by, rattling the windows. We sit year in, year out, watching the yellow sun warming the yellow bricks on the bank building. Plain, tidy brickwork. And just beyond it, the pink hotel with a white railing where Teddy Roosevelt stood. We drop sugar cubes in our coffee. They make a plop-plop sound. By 8 a.m., we stand and stretch and move out to our other lives, to the car repair on the main street, to the hardware store, to the cattle on the hill. Across the highway to the south of town, we hear the river doing what rivers do. And we cross the courthouse grass together before we splay out in separate lines.

THE TICK QUEEN

When Kathleen O'Neil was chosen as a finalist for Tick Queen, we all nodded our heads and said, "Well, of course, it would be Kathleen," because Kathleen wears such tight jeans and she has about eighty acres of land and she has flirted her way around every bend in the town to get to wear that crown with the foil Tick on the top. And we all watched the jars fill up with change, one in the tackle shop, one in the café, and one in the gas station, and there was Kathleen with her face smiling off of jar number 3, and men putting their money in, dropping in quarters like hailstones.

It wasn't jealousy, we said to ourselves, perhaps she deserved to wear her red flouncy formal and her long white gloves and sit on the fire engine beside the Tick King we preferred who, this year, was a rancher who donated money to build a pier on the reservoir which seemed, to us, a worthy endeavor and we put some of our nickels and dimes in his jar. Besides, we knew that to be the Tick Queen is such a public affair, and that if she won, Kathleen would go to Denver to meet the Governor. She would have her picture taken for the <u>Denver Post</u> with a satin ribbon across her breasts announcing her special status. We said to ourselves, perhaps she did deserve it. She had moved out here all the way from New Jersey and she bought a large ranch house and she had a pinto pony and a bay and a buckskin and she went to Denver and bought three new saddles when she moved in to town and she held a barbecue for the whole town at her house under the stars. And that was only last year when she saw the Tick Festival for the first time and talked us into letting her judge the baking competitions. We remember her standing on the side of the road and watching the fire engine go by with Janine Wetzler wearing that crown and Kathleen waving like she was really enjoying herself and we said that it was probably good for her to be in a town like ours instead of the East Coast with all that greed.

But at our weekly stitchery club we three agreed that this was a special honor, this Queendom, and it should go to someone who has rooted here because that was the metaphor, wasn't it? Tick fever, tick birds, tick disease—it's all about staying in one place and burrowing, isn't it? And maybe if Kathleen in her jeans would stay for a while, maybe she would earn the right to be a nominee instead of having Phil from the gas station nominate her and the rest of us having to stand there and listen to her tease and watch her smile and accept the honor as she brought out three professional and glamorous 8" by 10" photos of herself to be placed on the money jars. We heard her say what an honor it was to be a member of the royalty. And someone else said that if Phil has his way he might try to establish a rule where you can win it more than once, like the Triple Crown, and retire with three foil Tick Crowns, but someone else said that would never do because there are rules that say that, in terms of local history, it must be a different pair of people in the picture in the album for each year.

We three went so far as to look up the myths of ticks because we felt we should let her know the symbology. We drove from Beulah to the library in Colorado Springs and found an enormous dictionary from England so that we could see the names of mites that infest the hair or fur of animals such as dogs and cattle. We took recipe cards and wrote down all that we could find about bird-ticks and sheep ticks, ticks that cause havoc with calves and colts. We wanted her to know how a tick is a kind of louse and that, as a parasite, it can travel inside the wings of birds and can make big blue welts on horses. We wrote as quickly as we could, bending over the dictionary, trying to make out the Old World words. We listed any of the dipterous arachnids called ticks; we found mention of tick paralysis, paralysis caused by neurotoxin in the saliva of certain biting ticks; reminded her in our quick pencil script of tick pyaemia, a type of blood-poisoning in sheep, especially lambs, caused by staphylococcus aureus and leading to lameness or death. And we had gone through about fifteen cards when we summed it up by describing, as the dictionary taught us, tick disease characterized by a low mortality, with an incubation period of about four days, followed by a sharp rise in temperature and a period of fever. We ended with the fact that in areas of late lambing, abortions in ewes are sometimes attributable to tick-borne fever, and then we just lined up words on a card so that, read aloud, it sounded like a clock:

Dog ticks.

Horse ticks.

Tick birds

Tick seeds.

Tick spiders.

Tick typhus.

Ticia, said one.

Teke, said another.

Tyke, said the third.

And Tycke, Tike, Ticke, Tique. Tick.

We sent the cards to her in the mail the week before the election when we could see that her jar with her picture was almost full.

We waited.

We saw her around town at the grocery buying organic tomatoes.

We saw her laughing with Phil, drawing her hand across his chubby cheek.

We saw her in the tackle shop, garnering votes by asking about fly-tying.

We waited.

She didn't seem to care about the cards. She smiled at us as if nothing had come to her in her mailbox.

Sometimes we went to the shops where the jars were on the counter and waited for the clerk to turn his back and we reached in and took handfuls of change and dropped it in one of the other jars.

We knitted night and day on our Christmas stockings project, making variations of the reindeer with blue ticks. We crocheted baby afghans, pink ones with black, popcorn-sized tick spots, blue with black tick spots. We made a doll, stuffed it with straw, put a foil tick crown on its head and drove a handyman's nail through its heart. We placed it in the center of the table as we worked. It was wearing a red flouncy dress.

Mid-June, heading to the July festival, we had prayer chants as we stitched, making needlepoint tapestries with pictures of old fallen trees and tick eyes hiding in the crevices. Sometimes, at midnight, we went to the hills west of the reservoir and took off our clothes; and pressing our kitchen butcher knives, the handles tied with red ribbon, into the ground, we made a dancing circle where we swayed and leaped and sang, working our bodies into radiating energy, twirling in circles, our arms like propellers. Then we sat on the cold ground, sweat coating our flesh, and shared red wine and formed tick figures out of beeswax. We dug into the ground with our fingernails and buried the figures as we made humming noises, quiet murmurings about plague and disfigurement and tick fever. In the moonlight, we stood and dressed. As we pulled the knives out of the ground, we saw the earth bleed. We heard the earth gurgle and we saw white strands, filament fingers of maternal milk, running yellow in the light.

She won anyway.

On the Fourth of July, we three sat on the porch of the grocery, all puckered up, sipping lemonade as she rode by on the fire engine, throwing kisses and waving her gloved hands, that Tick Crown aglow with sunlight so as to blind a person. She was full of herself. Full as a tick. Her dark hair was flitting at her temples in the breeze. Beside her, the grey-haired pier donor in his paisley vest and string tie seemed younger than we had seen him.

We rocked on the porch, sipping our cold lemonade.
We listened to the ringing of the fire engine bell.
We rocked on our chairs, till we felt something rising in our bellies.

She has a pinto horse, said one of us.

And a bay, said another.

And a buckskin, said the third.

We rocked back and forth, back and forth, the lemonade all bittery on our tongues.

Teke, said one.

Tyke, and ticke, said another.

When shall we three meet again? Asked the third.

ESSAY FOR ENGLISH

Attached to this essay, as required by the assignment in English 12, you will find a photograph taken by a polaroid camera in the year 2003. This is a photograph of my sister and our dog Janus. It was taken almost 12 years ago by my mother. In it, if you look closely, you will see that my sister, who was 4 years old, and our black dog Janus are standing outside our house by the flower garden with yellow roses. You can see that Janus is big and thick. He is part Newfoundland and my mother brushed him all the time. There was always dog hair on the kitchen floor, like a carpet, in the evenings when my mother groomed him, pulling the steel-toothed brush along his sides, leaving tracks. Janus was an older dog when my sister and I were little. You can see in the picture that my sister, only 15 months younger than me, can touch the top of Janus's head, but only barely. I chose this picture for this essay because it holds Time. What you cannot see in the picture is that my sister is now 16, but what you can see is that, in the picture, she is frozen here at 4. I chose the picture because it was a happy moment. I was standing beside my mother who took the photograph. If you look, you can see two shadows, a long one and a shorter one, leading toward my sister and Janus. As she was taking the picture, my mother was talking to my sister and to Janus. And, if you look carefully, you can see that both of them are paying attention. My sister has blond pigtails. She is pretty like my mother. My sister has my mother's nose, a sort of pert nose, if that is the right word. But the important thing, the argument here, as you say, is what I know that you do not. The important thing is how a frozen polaroid picture can become a filmstrip, a string of mental pictures. Photographs do not hold still. They move You could say, no pun intended, they develop. A photograph is just a first frame.

To begin, I need to tell you that my mother loved Janus as much as she loved the rest of us. She bought Janus from a newspaper ad when she was first married. Janus was, you could say, the first child. There are other pictures of my sister and me when we were toddlers, lying on top of Janus, patting his nose, giving him some birthday cake. Those kind of pictures. We all have them. Anyway, my mother took Janus with us in the car wherever we went and Janus would wait in the car as we got school shoes at the mall. Janus would get tastes of McDonald's fries to eat as my sister and I fed him from our Happy Meals, dangling the potato strings over his head, all the way home. Janus was in our traditional Christmas cards, all of us sitting in front of the tree hung with tinsel bits and old ornaments, Janus plopped at the center of us, wearing a Santa hat or Janus soaking and dripping wet with sea water on our beach towels on our car trips to the ocean, or sitting with one of us on the sled, a big green scarf around his neck as my mother would always knit one for Janus when she finished ours.

What I know from this class, English 12, is that a picture is an artifact. I know that a subject stands there and the photographer aims the device at the subject. I know that light and dust drifts or emanates from the subject across space to the photography paper and collects. A photograph is a collection of light. It is evidence of a moment in Time. It is also cropped. There are things you will never know about this photograph of my sister and Janus with my mother's shadow unless I tell you. And something else. My neighbor told me that the best picture he ever saw of his mother was a picture taken of her when she was 5. He said in those days photographers would go door to door and take pictures of children or they would wander the beach and stop families or even bring a small pony with them. He said that this itinerant photographer, his word "Itinerant," stopped his grandmother and took a picture of his mother as a child in his grandmother's arms. He told me that he thought it was remarkable that a picture of someone as a child was a better resemblance of them than any other picture as they aged. It made me think that the picture of my sister with Janus may be like that. It may be the one I remember.

I have to say here, in a short rhetorical digression, that I have a friend named Rob, who is not in this English class, but who says things I try to remember, and I just want to say that Rob told me once that "dogs and balloons don't outlive you" and that I should remember that. And I did. I remembered it when Janus grew old and I would watch Janus taking much time to stand up. My mother said it was canine arthritis. She got some dog arthritis pills from our vet. Janus wobbled. Sometimes his back legs gave out. He whimpered until someone carried him up the stairs. Sometimes he cried if my dad tried to lift him to the backseat of the car. Sometimes I watched him just lie there, his head on his paws, refusing his food. This picture with my sister at age 4 and Janus at about 10 is important to me because of the Time theme. Janus is younger here, and, as I said, his coat in the picture is silky and thick.

I do not have pictures of Janus when his muzzle started to turn white, when he began to ache. I think my dad must have sorted through the shoe-box. And someone just took the pictures out of the albums. When Janus got old and wobbly, I remember that my father told my mother that we needed to put Janus down. He calculated Janus's age in dog years was 113. He said dogs expect that we will make that decision. He said it was what we should do. My mother said that she couldn't do it. And so Janus continued to sleep most of the day in the livingroom on the couch. At night my dad carried him upstairs and Janus slept between my parents on their bed.

If you go back and look at the picture of my sister and Janus, you will see that there is lots of summer light in the picture. My sister's yellow hair is becoming a sort of halo thing. The thing is, though, as you probably know, that polaroid film turns the whole picture yellow or sort of brownish. They do not make that film any more, or there is a warehouse where you can get some at a high price, but I do have to say that I miss the old polaroid film. When I was in 7th grade, I covered my walls with polaroid pictures of every-thing I did. I could see my life on the wall and I noticed it was slowly turning off-yellow, the edges of the pictures browning, the people dulling, if that is a word. I did not mind, though.

I want to say, now, at the center of my rhetorical argument, that pictures do not require cameras. I say this because I think that at indelible moments word pictures last longer than the real ones that might be taken out of the album or lost. If a picture survives, like a daguerreotype of a Civil War sol-dier on the ground, it is evidence, yes, but what is interesting to me is the way it gets translated into story. All pictures, I think, dissolve into words and, here is the irony, words are better when they are words about pictures. I say this because the picture of my sister and Janus should have this label: 'I am only going to say this once.'

Consider this word picture: You are upstairs in a dark house in your bed-room. You feel flannel pajamas. You hear wind in the old tree. You feel flannel and see dark and then you hear screaming down the hall, painful screaming in the dark. It is my mother. It is dark and flannel and screaming. I open my bedroom door and I see a crack of yellow and there is still the screaming and crying and I see the light and I see my father and he is carry-ing my mother in his arms down the stairs. He is holding her like a fireman holds a victim. He is rescuing her from something that is making her cry. I do not understand what. My father is holding her and opening the door and I can see the paramedics in green jackets on the porch. You watch how they take her and you hear as my dad calls up the stairs to me to get my sister and our coats and to shut the door to their room, to keep Janus from getting out, and to come with him. And now we are in the car and traveling behind the ambulance. The windshield makes a picture frame for the lights and the white ambulance with an orange stripe and red circling colors, all of it moving in black night.

I am 10 years old now. It is four years after the attached photograph. I enter the picture now. I translate. I have my hand around my sister to keep her warm. I do not hear any sound. I know it must be there. It is a graphic novel, quiet, this part a two-page drawing. Then a series of drawings of a hospital and nurses and doctors bending down to my mother's face.

Then I hear the words that become pictures. My father's voice. *Listen now, I am only going to say this once. Listen. Janus was asleep on the bed,* he is telling us, reminding us, he will only tell us this once, *and didn't we all know,* he is saying, *Janus's bones were bad, didn't we?* He says, *and, of course, we all knew that Janus was old and weak, and your mother,* he says, *your mother was sleeping and, in her sleep, your mother rolled over and touched Janus, maybe,* he says, *just a stray arm touch, an arm hitting Janus on the flank and Janus,* he says, *started up,* that's what my dad is saying, *Janus started up, and Janus growled and Janus, showing strength Janus did not have, lunged at your mother's face, and Janus bit your mother's nose almost off and pulled at her right eye and Janus tore the flesh around the eye, pulled out bits of bone, and bit at her mouth and growled and shook his head like he shook that stuffed lamb toy when he was young and Janus would not let go, shaking and tearing at your mother's face and,* my father says, *I pulled Janus from your mother, making Janus let go of our mother's head, and your mother's face was bleeding, like it was melting, and the nose was gone and her face ruined now and she was screaming and I carried her down the stairs and I want you to know that she will never look the same again.*

There was no camera. He made a picture spoken in past tense that we heard in present tense. He only said it once.

In the picture attached to this essay you can see my sister. She looks like my mother used to look. Her eyes are like my sister's, big and blue, and her hair yellow and her mouth sort of pouty. If you look at this picture, you can see my mother. Otherwise, it is more difficult to look at her.

Listen. I will only say this once: My mother's face is stitched together. Her nose is made of some sort of plastic material and her left eye pulls down on

39

to her cheek. Sometimes she must reach up to steady a twitching that comes to the muscles in her mouth. I watch her at the mirror as she brushes her hair. She looks at the brush. She looks at the barrette as she pulls her hair in place. My mother does not ever look at her face.

In conclusion, I hold that a picture is not a static thing. Sometimes I wake up in the night and see my father's story as a photograph. Sometimes I make a word picture where I am laughing with my friends and I see Janus on a sled with a green scarf. Pictures signify, as you said in class. They are evidence. They are bits of light and dust that attach themselves.

Here is my assignment for English 12, the photograph as argument. Attached is a picture of my sister and our dog Janus. The light is yellow. There are flowers. Janus is a big dog. My sister has a pouty mouth. My mother's shadow is at my sister's feet.

PROVENANCE

1.

My grandmother had no children, bore no flowers, as she phrased it. They found me secondhand at an orphanage in Pueblo, 60 miles to the north of Walsenburg, in Huerfano County, where they lived. I always thought of them, driving north through the flat prairie, all seabed, and seeing in the distance what looks like a big black steamship with tall smoke pipe masts, a ship rising on the dry land, up from the prairie floor. They found me in an orphanage in the town center where there is a pond and mallard ducks. I sat by that pond, a spindly thing, all elbows and a nose like a beak. They asked me what I cared about most in the world, and I said, "Quiet places." I told them I'd like a room where I could sit by myself and listen to my mind. I saw the man smile. He was a spindly thing, too, his smile only a thin crease in his face. He had on a white straw hat with a blue ribbon band and a wintry kind of suit like it was the only one he had. We sat by the pond. I brushed a brown feather I found over my knees. I closed my eyes and brushed my eyelashes. I lay back on the grass and stared at the sun. They told me they would stop by next week.

2.

My grandmother told me everything is secondhand, that I should remember that. Every pie or cut flower or story started somewhere else and surrendered itself. "Is that bird feather yours?" she'd asked. "Are your words yours or are you borrowing them?" I liked this really, this idea of hand-me-down everythings. I would stand and watch her in the bakery that they ran, white flour powdering her hair, her thick arms rolling out the dough like cloth and folding the edges of the breakfast buns so as to place the cherry jam or peach or raspberry in the center. "I learned this from my mother," she'd say. "Secondhand." And she would pass the fresh rolls over the counter to young mothers tired of the morning already or to railroad men just off shift. She'd bag them in brown paper. "Secondhand," she'd say to me as she took the dollar bills. She even said that was why I should call her "grand-mother." She said there was a mother somewhere, not here, and eventually whatever that word means to someone had to stay, so her title would be "grandmother" as in Eve, as in curiosity.

My grandfather, the spindly man, was called Jake. He ran the bakery, get-ting up at 3 a.m. to make the bread and doughnuts, letting my grandmother make the Napoleons and the Lady Baltimores and the butter cream icings for wedding cakes in the afternoon. After lunch he would walk me down to the river. I was only seven when I came to them, toting a tied up box with all my earthy possessions from the orphanage that she tucked under my bed, and so he held my hand gently as if I would break. He never said much as we walked. He just listened to the stream. Years later when he died, a quiet death, an aneurysm of some sort, we buried him in the cemetery in a plot closest to the river. I knew he loved the river. He told me once that rivers merely cycle and return. I thought he meant they go up and become clouds and rain down. He didn't. He meant they circle in time, moving all over the earth to come back. You can, he told me, step in the same river twice.

After dinner my grandmother would crochet, her hands like wild birds. I would sit beside her and watch the patterns come, cabled thumbs and chains of lace, like legions of memory at her command. Sometimes we would watch Lawrence Welk and that man with the accordion. It was the late 1950s and the dancers swirled or jitterbugged or waltzed and all of these soap bubbles filled the back of the stage. Sometimes we would just take an eve-ning stroll down the main street of town with its Duckwalls and its one bar and café and the movie theatre and pharmacy at the corner at the center turn to Alamosa. I liked the large plate glass windows of the dress shops and the way they drove new Fords into a main street building and put them on display. I liked the quiet, the way the windows of the shops reflected off of one another, the way I could see how the mannequins in flowered dresses on one side of the street appeared to be standing beside the 1958 two-tone Ford cars on the other.

Sometimes I think you know a town better when it isn't yours. If it's yours, you stop looking and you miss the cornices with Huerfano County A.1908 D. on the courthouse or the arched red sign of the Fireside Café or even the handprints in the cement of the main street dated 1931. Sometimes I think my grandmother understood that we must stand witness, secondhand witness, to see anything. Each Sunday she showed me Red Ryder cartoons in the Sunday newspaper, Red Ryder and his horse and his friend the Indian boy, and one summer Red Ryder came to town for the parade. That day she dressed me in blue jeans with the bottoms rolled and a white shirt with pearl buttons and a red cowboy hat and a beaded Indian belt she bought in Santa Fe on her honeymoon. She took me down to the courthouse lawn and there he was, the real thing, a good man, a smiling magazine type model man, but I had seen the other one, the art one with the square jaw and the horse with a wild eye, and I knew it was just as good. She took a picture of me there with her box camera. I was standing next to the Indian boy, Red Ryder is behind me but his head is cut off, and I can see she had curled my hair in sausage curls and pressed the hat down and tied it on with the white strings. Even in black and white you can tell the hat is red. And if you look closely, you'll see how my grandmother's shadow cuts into the picture. It rises at my feet and overwhelms me as I smile into the sun. In the picture her shadow almost covers half of my forehead where we seem to share one eye.

3.

My room was yellow. We lived over the bakery, Spanish Peaks Bakery, and I looked out over the side street that led to the school. She put a desk by the window and book shelves beside it on the wall and she lined the shelves with used copies of Nancy Drew and Cherry Ames and a volume of poems by Robert Louis Stevenson with a marker by "The Lamplighter." We were close to the school, but she walked me there every day. At three o'clock she'd be there near the fence waiting, watching the kids who lived miles away board the orange bus that went to La Veta and Ft. Garland. Hot August days she'd send Jake with me to Pueblo to buy shoes. He'd take me by the hand to the Buster Brown store where they let me stand in this machine and I could see my spindly toes turn green like sticks in the radiated light. Jake always picked sturdy shoes, the sturdier the better. "Choose quality," he'd say to me as he tucked the box under his arm. I remember sturdy red shoes with thick soles and plaid laces. I remember my grandmother's face when she opened the box. She had expected black patent leather shoes, girl's shoes, to go with white socks. "Oh, but Jake," she said with disappointment all over it, "these won't do. They're brogans." Brogans. I did not know what that meant. I said I liked them. She said they were going back. The only time I saw them fight was that time over shoes.

I thought about her voice when I was 10 and the shoe man came. His name was Mitchell, and he drove a used school bus filled with boxes of shoes. We didn't have to go to Pueblo, the shoe man came to us. He stopped in front of the library in August and in May. He stepped down the stairs and stood in the sun in a starched shirt with blue suspenders and grey trousers. He stretched and wiped his brow and shifted his back muscles. He reached back and drew out his suit jacket and put it on even in the hot sun. I could tell he was a clever man, a man from somewhere in the north, Cheyenne, maybe, or Ft. Collins, somewhere with cottonwood trees, north. He had a route. He'd taken the seats out of the bus and replaced them with shelves. He kept one row of seats for customers to sit and try on the shoes, and he had workboots and black Mary Janes and baby shoes and thick walking boots with laces of every color. He had cowboy boots and spectator pumps. He had large metal gadgets to measure the toes, and he had a smile that said he'd met you before, even if he hadn't.

I was helping my grandmother with the vanilla pudding when she turned by chance and saw him out the window with his bus. She knew him, I could tell. Her face went still, her eye cold.

"Mitchell," was all she said.

"Do you know him?"

"Did once—a long time ago. He hasn't been around for years."

"Does he sell brogans?" I asked, saying the word, borrowing it.

"He'll sell you whatever you want."

She turned back to the pudding, to the Napoleons. I watched the man tip his hat to the passersby. He had dark black hair and eyes that matched. He was not spindly. He seemed to care about every person who crossed his path.

By my count, Mitchell was in town for only three hours, fanning himself with his hat, smiling, then closing the bus and drifting to the café for dinner. Thin sliced beef, mashed potatoes, I imagined, with buttery green peas. Then, he walked up the street, stepped into the bus, ground the clutch, and headed north to make it to Stem Beech or Colorado City before night. I watched him at the window, memorizing the thick oil of his head, even the sweat moons under his arms. My grandmother never looked up all afternoon. She made profiteroles as if she knew there would be a run on them.

In the evening I asked her, "You knew him when he was a young man?" but she did not look up from her crochet, her hands just moved and the squares of yellow and blue came out like ordered windows. Jake was asleep. He went to bed around 7:30 to get up by 3 a.m. for the bread. He never heard our evening talks.

"Yes."

"Handsome?"

"Yes."

"He make you laugh?"

"Not me, in particular."

"Who, then?"

"Someone. Blond girl."

"Friend of yours?"

"Not so much."

"He sell her what she wanted? Anything she wanted?" I borrowed her words.

"You could say that." And she put down the yarn and turned on the Lawrence Welk show. She did not look my way. "Goodness, those bubbles, those bubbles," was all she said.

Her reticence stayed with me. I'd see him twice a year only, Mitchell. He never seemed to age, but I knew he had to, all that driving, all those plates of café mashed potatoes. I saw him about eight times altogether, the last time in the week before Jake died, one Sunday afternoon in May. After the funeral my grandmother and I sat by the kitchen table. The people had gone. We had casseroles with green beans and mushroom soup lined up on the counter and foil-wrapped lasagnas and loaves of homemade bread, someone feeling that we probably couldn't make it ourselves for a while.

My grandmother didn't cry. It was as if she felt we'd just borrowed Jake a while from some big lending library, like we're all on some layaway plan. She sat at the table and sipped her coffee with milk. She looked out the window at the back of our lot that faced the school. She reached up once in a while and patted the top of her hair as if to tame the humidity that made it lift away from her face.

"When I'm gone," she said. "You can tell them that Mitchell killed him."

"The shoe man?" I couldn't believe it. "But, Mitchell wasn't even here. Jake died in his chair watching some program on lions."

"It was Mitchell just the same," she said. "Mitchell. You can tell them after I die,"

4.

What I know is that the base of life, if there is one, is memory. Sometimes nowadays I like to watch that program, "The Antiques Roadshow," because, I think, it proves my point every Wednesday from 7 p.m. to 8. My grandmother liked it, too. She lived well into her 80s and we would sit in her livingroom on an overstuffed couch she bought as a newlywed in 1948. She liked the odd children's banks of heavy iron with firemen and fire brigade horses. She liked the turquoise glaze vases from Van Briggle Pottery because she knew that that Van Briggle man came to Colorado for a tuberculosis cure in 1915. It wasn't the items, the dragonfly brooches or the German stuffed bears with glass eyes, that intrigued her so much as the stories of dying aristocrats who passed paintings on to scullery maids or Vermont ladies who found that their cherry pie plate dated from the Revolutionary War. My grandmother said that provenance is the only meaning, the pie plate was just clay unless you knew who touched it.

I suppose I agree with her to an extent, and I think that provenance, the original owners, may make a difference, but in the end it is desire that presses us to collect things. I say it is all desire, surfaces that pull us in like trout. Somehow, I say, our eye meets a pattern that we recognize inside of us, the twist of a branch, the geometry of a tile, the red color of a jewel, and the object replicates the abstraction already there, inside. We see an inner self turned out in surface design. It is not aesthetic or historic or intellectual. It is a moment of desire, a feeling of water running in the self, a wallowing. In the end, I say, we collect what we are.

5.

I only learned the story secondhand. My grandmother never told me. I learned it from the mother of a friend at school, this tale of how Mitchell killed Jake. It did, as my grandmother hinted, involve a blond girl. Her name was Herta. She was Latvian, all yellow-white hair and cheekbones that made promontories under her eyes. Her uncle brought her here days after the war when he could find her. She was only 17 when she arrived, but she had stood witness to the hanging of her husband at the hands of the Nazis. The soldiers made her watch him die, forced her to make memory of their power, engraved in her that the world is a vale of monstrosities. Her uncle sent money to his brother, and the family somehow managed to get her out of Latvia to Walsenburg where they ran a pharmacy. Herta worked there with her cousins. She spoke no English when she came, but her eyes were a source of consolation for everyone in town after the war. None of us, everyone in town would say, would ever know the suffering that Herta knew, watching a young boy, suspended like a catalpa pod, swinging in the light breeze, his feet moving in small gravitational circles.

Jake was a devoted disciple, age 18 years, at the pharmacy. He bought band-aids and aspirin that he didn't need. Sometimes in spring, he merely took her a hand picked bouquet of lilacs. "Purple stars," he would tell her, speaking slowly. "Constellations." I wondered if he ever walked with her by the river or if he taught her, as he did me, about the magnetism of the sun when we found our separate spots and lay down on our backs on the bank, our arms stretched like birds, when we let the yellow sun fade into us and let the earth give us her magnetism, that's what Jake called it, "getting our magnetism." Sometimes I hope he didn't teach her that. I hope he saved it just for me.

My grandmother watched the courting, watched it all. She was not married to Jake then, but she cared about him. She worked in the Duckwall's behind the counter, and she would see him go by the window, lilacs in his hand going one way, pharmacy sacks coming back. Sometimes on her break she would cross the street just to stand in the pharmacy and listen to the townspeople honor Herta in their own way, speaking slowly and loudly, asking for cold elixirs or cough syrup as if the words were new in this world.

If Herta chanced to come to Duckwall's to buy yarn in winter or flowered material from the bolts in the back in summer, my grandmother merely took the yarn or the fabric, tapped in the price on the cash register and took her money. No funny words. No smile. No field of grace. My grandmother merely noted the girl's brogans, the sound thick leather soles made as Herta went out the door.

When summer came that year, everyone could see Jake was smitten. My grandmother knew it, too. She would see him leave his father's bakery at 5 p.m. and cross the street to wait for her so he could walk her home. Quiet boy. Latvian girl. Lilacs or wild flowers. The girl, looking down at the flowers, her head bowed to their color. The young man walking at her elbow, his eyes looking defensively ahead to some future down the cement.

6.

I have these albums, black pages with black and white pictures, with the white ruffled edges. I have pictures of people I do not know. She left them to me. They intrigue me with their momentary opaque worlds, faces looking at me, or rather at somebody I have become in the moment I look, the picture taker, faces that make me into the gazer. In them I see life in bits, like daubs of paint. I read the albums like a text of posed worlds, for in these old books, there are no candid or random tellings. People stand in knowing states, assured that the world is what they know it to be. There they are at holiday tables, at vacation sights with signs telling the elevation, at tombstones. And they are glued in to the books in sequence, fixed with white or black photo corners, bits of secured time. They age in the turning of these pages and they disappear. Even the ones who did the gluing disappear. And the album comes into the hands of relatives or neighbors or antique roadshow sorts who make it into history or economics. All that assurance in the eyes of the lady in the belted 1940s dress or the bride in the white satin, all that freshness, twisted like a sugar beet in the ground, to the scrutiny of the unknowing.

This is how I see this picture I never saw. It is a grey day, in black and white, but you can tell it is summer. Mitchell is there, ten years younger, 1947 this time, smiling. He is standing by his bus with all the shoes, leaning on the hood and wearing a light grey suit and suspenders and a bow tie of a dark color, perhaps a navy blue. The sun is at noon, at peak, no shadows, all is quiet, nothing moves except one haunting white haired girl in a flowered grey skirt, in black and white, butter yellow maybe with green flowers in my version, as she lifts her chin to laugh at something Mitchell has just said. She has on a white blouse, that Mexican fiesta style they sell in Santa Fe, that pulls off the shoulders, and the sun is hot, and her face lifts to him like it would to an altar figure in her church. There is no album picture like this, but I suspect my grandmother made the image often in her mind. Her silences passed it all to me. Then, as I see it, they were gone. He touched her face, maybe. He spoke quietly as he might gentle a skitterish horse. He said words like "Denver. Cheyenne. Laramie. Yellowstone." And the girl who watched her passionate young husband, feet and arms tied back, swinging in the air like a pendulum, like a flour sack pulling downward, decided to let herself know unbridled freedom, out of the cage, away from the faces gazing at the windows. The way I see it she got in the bus. They went north. He had a route. He would take her where the cottonwood trees stretched their long, turgid roots, where water was easy. He would dress her up, give her red leather shoes, take her to restaurants with singers at the microphone, call her "Doll" like those men did in the movies. It was desire, you see. She had stepped in the same river twice.

7.

My grandmother believed a person could die of a broken heart. She said that at her wedding to Jake, in 1948, she had taken his hands at the Episcopal church and his hands were like dead fish, cold, cold. He had smiled at her, she said, but she could see that his mind was somewhere else and the smile was more of a "thank you" than a happiness smile. She said they both knew that she had rescued a shy and spindly man from a life of loneliness. Of course, she knew she had planned this moment, making Lady Baltimores and Napoleons in her mother's kitchen and taking them down to the bakery for him to taste, watching his eyes as he bit in to her eclairs, brushing powdered sugar from his mouth as he consumed her delicate sponges with vanilla cream between the layers. She seduced him with fillings, raspberry and lemon. She courted him with mousses lathered between chocolate slabs of cake. Trust pudding, she told me. Trust pudding.

She got him secondhand. I have the picture, black and white. She is posed by a rosebush, and her suit, by my guess, is light blue. Her face is round under her hat, her hair trying to pull out from underneath it. She is holding a bouquet of wildflowers, standing beside her awkward groom who is squinting at the picture taker. It must be noon. There are no shadows. The sun is not in his face, yet he is squinting. I see no magnetism here.

But when I consider Mitchell with that Herta by his side, I can hear their laughter in that bus as he teaches her the names of cities on the road: Stem Beech and Rye and Longmont and Windsor and Greeley and Eton and Virginia Dale. They ride with her sitting on the customer seat in the front and the boxes of shoes shifting and swaying against each other. Sometimes he pulls off a dirt road somewhere by Colorado City and they make love in the bus, lying on a quilt on the floor. Sometimes he takes her to dinner for steaks at restaurants on Colfax in Denver where women in long red gowns sing songs like "Shrimp Boats are a'comin, There's dancing tonight." Sometimes they splurge on a motel, buying only storebought bread and cheese and wine to have in their room. And they have a system. When they arrive at a point on the route, he lets her off on the edge of town or at a park with picnic tables, telling her he'll be back in just three hours. In small towns, he tells her, it is better that he show up alone. He needs to make the customers laugh, he says. Flirt a bit when you come right down to it, he says. She nods. She understands. She sits on the park bench in the shade, tracing her finger along the flowers on her skirt. She is happy. She listens to the birds. She watches the wind touch the wheat stalks. She hums songs about shrimp boats. Sometimes she closes her eyes and, suddenly, the boy she used to know is swinging from the tree.

Of course, they stopped coming to Walsenburg for a few years. Mitchell cut it from the route. The only school buses down the main street had farm children looking from the windows. Parents had to drive to Pueblo or Trinidad to get school shoes. No one knew what happened to them. Her uncle never said her name. People started talking normally at the pharmacy, ordering ear drops and leaving. Jake got up every morning at 3 a.m. and made doughnuts. Each day he made more doughnuts than he made words.

8.

There is a white edged picture of my grandmother and Jake and me coming out of the orphanage. I'm holding my box of things, tied shut. My hair is in pigtails. I am ten years old. They are ten years married. Over the steps of the old brick dormitory are the words, "We are bound as children dancing." I remember that in the car as we passed Stem Beech on the way to Walsenberg, my grandmother turned to the back seat where I sat, wearing blue shorts and a white blouse, and she said, "Huerfano County. That's where we live. Huerfano, pronounced 'Wherefano' means 'orphan' in Spanish." I watched the blue peaks rising on the side of the road. I saw a few stray cows, a pinto horse, but mostly sagebrush, dry land. We passed the steamship that was the iron works and 60 miles down the road turned off to Walsenburg, the road rising past the Hill Top Motel of white adobe and down past the middle school and stucco houses and county seat, across the railroad tracks to the bakery. There is another picture of us in front of the bakery on that same day. I don't know who took the picture, but there at our feet sits a dog, a white dog, in black and white. I would learn, in time, that he was the town wanderer. Everyone fed him. Stray dog, probably. Huerfano.

9.

She came back on a Thursday in the fall, sixteen years after she had left, 1963. I was in high school and on counter duty at the bakery that Thursday afternoon in October. The air was finally autumn cool, leaves were slipping from the few trees in town. The Greyhound bus pulled in and stopped, and I watched as she got off, a woman I had never seen before. She was a bloated thing, filled with water, her face puffy and red and unwell. She wore an old wool coat and a cotton dress, and her shoes were odd, old fashioned, sort of 1940 pumps, red. Her hair was white, pure white, and thin around her face. I watched her. I was the only one there. She picked up a black suitcase and walked to the pharmacy. I felt this chill, I remember. She was otherworldly, dragging that suitcase like some ghostly silt ready for another journey.

Her uncle took her in, nursed her, gave her back the color in the white ashen face. She commenced to work at the pharmacy again. My grand-mother only said, "So, Herta's come back from her travels." I knew my grandmother went to the pharmacy for more than one reason, everybody did, buying St. Joseph's aspirin and band-aids and toe pads for corns. I sus-pect she took time to examine the ruin of a thing this woman had become, so thick, her fingers larger that the rings she wore, a turquoise stone on one hand, a silver band on the other, her dress belt cinched at the last hole, her blue eyes like small blue plums pressed in dough. I suspect my grandmother just handed her the pills and paid, and, later, as the winter snows came and she had adjusted to the haunted soul who sold medicines, my grandmother held a bag with cough syrup in one hand and her change in the other, the snow whirling past the window, and looked into the woman's eyes and said, "Jake's dead," and walked away, a bell jangling at the door. I suspect she was stern in her pronouncement about the dead made to the almost dead.

Now, this is secondhand, but the town said that Mitchell kept her only as long as she was pretty and he wore her out with babies that they abandoned across the western states. Babies cannot live in school buses and motels, he told her; and she had to agree. They say he kept her in that bus like a Rapunzel in a tower for years. Then he set her down somewhere in Kansas where she lived alone, a beauty in decay, until her arms thickened and her body filled with juices and gravity pulled at her breasts and stomach. Then, I suspect, she felt that something was wrong inside her and she came back to set it right. Everyone in town said it was an infection of the womb, of that vulnerable and desirous place inside her where she dropped babies like a ewe. I said it was probably the heart. In towns like ours, it's usually the heart. Whatever part it was, she kept going, shuffling around filling prescriptions in old house slippers with run down heels, her feet thick, her ankles and legs all one column. She was focused and efficient. She was all white, her skin, her hair, her blouse and her pharmacist's coat, and we all thought she was getting better.

It was about the time that I graduated from high school that the chain store, Safeway with an inside pharmacy, moved in on the edge of town, and her uncle felt he must give up his drugstore. She said she would help him as he helped her. She would make his store a cottage industry, a thrift store, a collectibles shop, and so, to me, she became a paradox. It was odd, I thought, to fill the shop with things nobody wanted, white elephants. Odd, to try to make the castaway item significant, desirous. She would go down the Walsenburg alleys and find abandoned things. She would take the bus to Pueblo to go to the Salvation Army. She could gather anything the library abandoned at its yearly sale. And she did fill that room. She had old Christmas ornaments and coffee thermos bottles and glass cats and toasters. She had costume jewelry and fiesta ware plates and floor lamps with glass bowl tops. She had horseshoes and an elk head with glass eyes. She had old pillows made of cheap satin with the state of Nevada stenciled on the center.

And we all knew she sat in the corner, breathing from her spongy lungs and waiting for someone to enter the big dark place to buy a ceramic dog or a straw hat or a cotton handkerchief with pink roses. Mostly, though, you could tell she just watched us over the counter, over the abandoned things. I could feel her on my skin. I knew she was there behind the jewelry cases where she kept the gold casket boxes made of pot metal, the Indian necklaces and beaded belts. As I circled, looking at the plastic flowers or the silverware in shoe boxes, her lungs pulled hard in the dust, in the musky odors of the shadowed room. In the darkness of her shop, she stopped wearing white. She chose a silken black dress with shoulder pads, loose in the bodice, belted, the style of the 1940s. I do not know where she got it. And she started to dye her hair a sheeny black to match the dress, in time forgetting to freshen the color, letting it grow white at the roots like a thin field of autumn snow.

Once I bought a small plate from her. It said "Czechoslovakia" on the back. I saw her eyes were watering, the pupils becoming foggy, but she wore no spectacles. Perhaps, I thought, she kept the room dark because the light hurt her eyes.

"Cookie plate," that was the only phrase I ever said to her.

She nodded. She wrapped it in newspaper and put it in brown paper tied with string.

10.

The box under my bed all these years is wrapped in brown paper and tied with string. It is the box I carried out of Pueblo that day long ago, the box I am holding in the picture with the stray dog. It was wrapped that way when they handed it to me and for a while my grandmother placed it high on a shelf in the linen closet. One day she took it down and said, "Perhaps we should open this now. It could tell you who you are." I said I knew who I am. She put the box under my bed.

I am told there is a theory in physics, something called Schroedinger's Cat. The theory says that given a box with a radioactive element, a Geiger counter, a flask of poison, and a cat in it, and given the possibility that the element might decay and set off the counter that would spill the poison and kill the cat, you must always assume the cat to be dead and alive. You must allow for the possibility of the particle or the cat being in two states at one time. I understand that theory. Whatever is in that box is dead and alive to me until I open it. It is a collection, perhaps a pair of baby shoes, a letter in some language I do not know, a confession of desire. Perhaps there is a photograph with white edges, a red ribbon for my hair, a golden ring. When I think of the box, I know only possibility.

We fill our wombs as best we can.

The owl, they say, was a baker's daughter.

AFTERLIFE

West of town, the hillside pasture becomes a parking lot two times a year, for the pageant we do in July, the one about the massacre of 1879, and for the sheep dog trials in September, the one that attends to pattern. The people come and press in against the mountain and the ceremony layers in like mica bits that shine in the light and break.

It being September you can watch the handlers with their dogs. They work against time in the meadow. The sheep are over the hill, a mile, a half a mile, and the handler sends the black and white dog out there where he can't see it, but it knows to find the sheep and begin the fetching. The sheep are dirty, stupid even, but fear gives them intelligence. Some cluster near the others, twisting, changing direction, a wild eye on the dog with his ears pricked, his front shoulders down, his butt in the air. Sometimes the sheep run, scattering down the hill, leaping with some erratic surge. Sometimes they just stop, unaware of the people watching, and munch the grasses. But, then, the dog is there, a god of dark dominion, its blue eye vigilant. And the handler works the dog, a silver whistle in his mouth, the sound a sort of "wheet" of a small bird, and everything is a copper engraving, backwards, dog moves left, handler's right; dog away, dog down, dog come by. And he works time, calming the dog, keeping it moving, keeping it from leaping at the sheep, from biting the wool, from the judge calling "That'll do," dismissing the team with a breath. And they work mind to mind like elastic stretches between them, like a string of silk that crochets and holds, twists back and knots. And the September sun is hot on the hill and the dog's tongue is loose in its mouth, its flanks wet with sweat. And the dog is running, running, reversing, cutting away, answering human mind without debate.

I know this because I work the three days of the show selling funnel cakes in a tent on the hill. September comes and with it the dog trials and the small tent with a side table for the batter mixture and the stove with the hot oil. I sell funnel cakes all day. It's not just a morning thing. Funnel cakes are desire, thick doughy circles of batter that float on the oil like sacraments, a circular ring of metal to set the boundaries, dough that piles up on itself like a topographical map, dough frying to a golden color and presented on a paper plate. I just ask customers if they want cinnamon and my uncle behind me, wearing his red baseball cap, starts the dough. I smile and tell the people in the line that powdered sugar is requirement, but cinnamon is grace.

The cakes sell for $4.00 and my uncle eats two an hour all by himself, and I find myself running to the ticket booth for change, and sometimes I take a moment to listen to the announcer describing to the crowd how a lady from Encino, California who had made it into the semifinals was now choosing to walk away, to withdraw the young dog who had made the final cut. I hear a man on the benches telling his wife how the dog went out toward the sheep, a mile away, and turned the wrong direction, moving low and long, a stalker, but moving the wrong way, her whistle confusing him. Just too young, the man says, pup of a dog, stopping and lying low, moving toward the roadside, moving east as the five sheep sat on the hill in the west, pup of a dog, green in the world.

I hear it all as I walk past the other tents, past the old man from the Middle East who sells wooden Russian dolls that nest inside dolls and dark polished brooches painted with girls in sleighs being drawn over the snow mountains. I nod to the lady with Indian silver bracelets, to the Peruvian lady with llama statuettes, to the photographer who comes from Southern Colorado with picture after picture of yellow aspen and purple columbine, and to my old high school art teacher who makes ceramic pots. I see him wave and his eyes study my eyes as I notice that this time he has made everything a sort of dark blue. This year, at the July pageant, his signs said, "Portuguese Yellow" and now, in September, "French Blue" in handprinted cards on shelves of butter dishes and sugar and creamers and bowls that are pools of ink. I notice how fragile he is, how his skin is thin paper and how when the sun shines on him from the side, he is almost transparent, his nose reddish like someone is holding a flashlight to it, revealing the bone inside like the spine of a silver fish. He mouths some words, but I hear no sound, just a quiet sigh, then he offers up a sort of smile, all crooked and Christlike, and I know he is watching even the corners of my mouth as I study the pots. I know he is trying to see the pots reflected in the iris of my eyes. Sometimes as I pass I touch his French Blue casseroles and I glance at the display rack in the corner, at the dark blue covered bowl, the lid off center, the handles like small alert ears lifted on a dog who has heard a strange noise.

Then I move off with a wave, a lift of my hand, to the ticket booth just as the announcer on the loudspeaker is telling the audience not to bring pet dogs to the dog trials next year. He is explaining that, at this moment, a family's dog named Dick with one blue eye and one black eye is lost on the mountain. I hear him, his voice metallic and angry, threatening that next year they will charge $100.00 per dog should anyone bring in a pet collie or bulldog or poodle that might lose itself.

I've watched the border collies in the ring so many times. It's a dance, the partners miles from each other. It's a knowing in the mind and ear. The dog chooses the human, gives up its native tribe for the human voice, for the hand on the head, for the riding in the truck or the sleeping in the camper or the oasis trough filled with water, cold water, a bath after the fifteen minutes of sun work. The dog honors the game. He sees the sheep with the orange bands and cuts them out. Shed Two. He prowls and intimidates and turns the sheep about, calmly, so they enter the white pen. He restrains in the name of pattern.

There comes a moment when the crowd hushes and the sheep are at the center of the ring and the shedding begins. I can hear the quiet even over that snakelike sound, the batter and oil, the shaping going on. I can see the tension in the backs of the people on the benches, the man who sells ceramic clay-houses, and the Pizza Palace lady whose husband died last spring, and the taciturn man who owns the old hotel with its lobby walls covered with heads of deer and elk, twenty or thirty of them, beasts with sproutings of antlers and brown glass eyes that watch us. I can see the section where the veterinarians sit, old men mostly, horse doctors, large animal vets, who are ironed and suspendered and bedabbled with pearl buttons on their cowboy shirts.

Sometimes I watch them and I consider all those dead animals watching people at the hotel and all those men watching here and my friend Nick whose eyes were the color of those French Blue pots, Nick, somewhere studying to be a doctor of animals, away at school for three years, and, there on the benches, his father, like Nick, one who studies knowing, and Nick just like him, assisting somewhere, putting salve on sores, clipping toenails, putting down old cats, doing that something, he said, because we often do that something, that pattern we've watched all our lives. And Nick long ago watching his father's hands, his touching of a cat as he would touch a woman, his pulling of a calf into the cold on an April morning, steam coming from its body in strings.

So you'll go to vet school? I asked him that spring with the crabapple trees all white.

Yes.

Come fall?

Yes.

I shall feel the absence.

There is no such thing.

That's what he said, I remember. There is no such thing.

But that was two springs ago, with white crabapple blossoms, and my uncle planting Early Girl tomatoes and Brandywines that would, come September, turn giant red with skins so thick that sometimes I'd watch him peel them and stand at the sink with a salt shaker and eat them in extended bites, red juice dripping down his wrist. That was spring and this is September now, and the Palisade peaches are gone from the baskets at the farmer's market, all pulled away from the orchards of Eden out Highway 70. Elsewhere.

And sometimes I know I live in a state of absence, that this place on the Western Slope is an afterlife. I think of the oceans that filled the land and the flutes of earth they left like silverware lined up in a drawer and I think of what crawled out of the water and died and was pressed in stone like I used to press lace into the clay in art class, of things incised into matter. In July, always, when we do the pageant about the massacre that happened on these hills, I think of the incising inside me, inner fossils that I note and hold and memorize.

And I think of that girl, that Meeker girl, Josie, who lived here, and how she knew, as I do, that places make their claim and Josie's claim was here in a house up from the river not far from the dog arena where she must have stood by the window that day and watched the Indians across the river as they were dancing. In the September cold they were dancing and there was mist rising and the steady sound of their song and, behind her, her father paced, Bible in hand, reading the Psalms outloud and she saw the Indians coming up from the water, riding hard with weapons, and she saw them bring fire to her house and strike her father and shoot a bullet in his head and drive a barrel stave down his throat and Josie watched and was made into pattern here, on this ground, turning in her place in the swirl, like a frozen ammonite, the hem of her dress dragging the floor with a paper sound of old leaves, becoming the pattern that we call Josie Meeker and that we tell in the summer, in our pageant when someone becomes Josie, wrapped in a wooly shawl, and the Indians come and she and her mother and Flora Ellen Price are carried away.

In July we build Josie's house out of cardboard and paint it brown like a log cabin and we have a farmer dressed as Meeker, the Indian Agent, who argues, holding his Bible to the sky, with other farmers dressed as Indians, proclaiming to them about horse racing on the Sabbath, about the gambling and the drinking. And in the July summer heat, draped in a black wool shawl, Josie watches as her father takes a plow and presses it in the earth in long lines, cutting the Indians' pony racing track, its snow and rocks upturned, pressing his mark, his ethical argument, incising himself for time to come. Behind him we place long stretches of butcher paper and paint the backdrop with solid blue mountains and white snow and we draw in lines to mark the ruts of the wagons pulled by horses. Sometimes we paint in flowers that were never there in late September, bits of red and yellow against all that whiteness, seasons overlapping like funnel cake threads. And sometimes I know Josie never left. She watches from the hill, even as I watch in the hot sun and a black and white dog brings the sheep down the hill and through the center gate, a group of five. And she admires the dog as it maneuvers them toward the announcer booth, around its handler and up to the left gate. She watches as the dog stops, cautious, still, its tongue a ribbon at the corner of its mouth. She sees as it controls, shifts them over to the gate, to the shed ring where two ewes have to be separated from the others. Josie knows. Josie understands the way it turns on a moment's choice by a frightened animal. The sheep, you see, just want to stay together. Just there, head to foot, bundled in wooly terror.

The Indians took her. I told you that. And I think about her. And I think about the listening and the call and the trust of not seeing, but knowing. And I consider her as I press lace into clay and pull it up slowly to see the grace, the definition of something lyrical, some dance or heat of movement in unmoving matter.

So you'll go to vet school? I said.

Yes.

Come fall?

Yes.

I shall feel the absence.

There is no such thing.

That's what he said. There is no such thing.

I want you to know the way things work at the end. The difficult part of the trials, if you watch, is this final part, the penning. The handler can move and use his body and his crook to make an extended self—the gate, the rope, the handler with his stick, making a fourth wall, an illusion, so the sheep see the stitched-together barrier as a solid line. And the dog works. And the handler moves his stick up and down and the sheep watch. And when they're in place, the handler reaches for the rope and stretches his arms like wings. And the dog circles and circles and the clock runs and all trust that something will move them to mold, that something—even if it is terror, will make them group, make them come to one mind after all that scattering. And the handler and the dog, invaders, really, intend the consummation before the time runs out.

And sometimes when I see that happen, I consider Josie Meeker, yellow-haired. I think about the cold that filled her blood. Josie, the pretty one. Josie, the one her father fawned upon, the one whose hair he petted in the sunshine when she was small. I consider the Indian eyes studying her, their brown-eyed focus on her palomino self, looking hard at the shape of her nose, the small earlobe. I know that when the Indian's theft of the women was over, when they were returned, Josie never spoke about it. Her sister

Rose did, and the mother. They toured the mountain towns explaining the outrage of the weeks with the Indians. And Josie, she sat at home, mute as a fish, all that yellow hair fading to pale ecru, her hands moving in crochet patterns. Wrapped in some black wooly shawl, I think she must have made a noise, a moan perhaps, a sounded syllable of air, suggesting vacant absence, even if there is no such thing.

LUCY

I shall look for the cell of the work. I think it is contour and not detail. It is no longer photographic detail. It is black and white. It is flatness. It is a third space. I will hear it, not just see it. I will combine it. I will trace it from what my hand wants. If my father dies, I shall not go to the funeral as I will be looking for it.

Is it a black crow?

Yes.

Is it a white hill?

Yes.

Must I watch it come from the black liquid?

Yes.

Will I see it?

Sometimes, not always.

Is it too late for the gods?

Yes.

಼

I study the art books at the library in Steamboat. No one looks at them but me. They sit on the shelf, spines still golden, engraved letters that say Cezanne and Manet still cut with tight edged precision.

But I prefer the pictures in old albums of photographs, the stiffness in the 19th century bodies, the overlays and folds of clothing made for winter. The people are waxy mannequins with wiggy hair and frozen legs. They are dead people photographed leaning on planters or sitting in velvet chairs, their fingers become claws.

The only way I knew my mother was from the albums of relatives she left, soft velvet ones with "Souvenir" on the top, a hard and plastic one with a rose etched in a vanilla drapery. She had one with all the photos from Council Bluffs, Iowa. One from a ranch somewhere near Meeker, the women in culottes riding horses and one, a school class sitting outside a redstone building, a dog at their feet.

My father told me that I must memorize my mother's face. As the mother lay dying, he lifted me, his only daughter, for me to watch the labored breathing and to see the fevered cheeks, the vacancy. Even then my eye moved from the mother's face to the pillow and she could see the way the crocheted case made geometry.

"A mother is not metaphor," he told me.

&

I buy an instamatic camera with twenty-four pictures. I take my father's horse and ride uphill behind the house toward the stream at timberline. I try to take the picture while the horse walks, hoping for a blurring. I lean down to get part of the horse's neck in the picture so that it blocks out a portion of the land. I dismount and then get on the saddle backwards to get the horse's rump and the road. I gentle the horse and take a picture of its glassy eye reflecting the distorted me with the camera.

When we are at the widest part of the stream, I lean off the horse and try to photograph a trout waiting in a quiet pool. I lay down on the ground and take photos of the yellow aspen leaves and the stalks of flowers. I put the camera close to the stones on the riverbed, so close that the rock face is a full-frame of speckled sky.

When I have twenty-four shots, I ride the horse back to town and walk down the hill to turn the film in at Spiro's store. I wait a week to get the pictures back, turning in my next film cartridge, taking the week-old prints.

I take them to the Colorado bar and spread them out four at a time. I sort the ones I want to draw. I can feel The Fox looking at them sideways. He taps on the corner of the ones he likes and hopes I might draw.

"Ever think of using color film?" he asks as he looks at the rolls of grey aspen and maples, the grey horse rump, a grey dog on a grey porch.

I do not answer. He's asked the question before. We both know it is rhetorical.

∞

A photograph is an image of death. The thing sends out its light and it touches some chemicals and affixes the fact that it was there once in time, but then, the thing as it sits there is caught in other light and other poses. Because the photograph holds it all so still, I can make the cross-stitch on a button have its place against a shirt. I can work the scratches in the leather of a boot, the jowly layers of the face.

I will, though, no longer make the threads so perfect.

What will you do instead?

I will attach them to the things that stand around them.

To what end?

I will show that one is many, one only in the many.

But separate, too?

No.

And what is this white square then with a circle in the center?

Something not a metaphor.

ౡ

I would like to remain with meanings. I will not replicate. I will become the impression. I will transform the button before the time comes to withdraw.

Here is the line. It moves up the curve of the mare's neck and turns to become the bough of the evergreen and down to the stones and water where it curls around an impression, dark and mottled, and comes back to the grey neck to attach itself again to the twist of the grey cloud in the grey sky and off and down again to water, but not.

What will you do with this one?

The photograph with the blur?

Yes.

Wipe my ink line a wet cloth on the paper.

To what end?

Time.

I am turning now and cannot return. I pose them with a drapery. I put in the Hamms beer sign, that eternal water running over rocks, that space of neon tubing, an upper edge, a heaven. I find a pedestal for him to lean on, put her in a fancy chair with roses carved against her shoulders. I draw the line. I ink in the vanishing point.

ౡ

It will be a continuous black line with bumps.

It will be a container.

Of sorts.

ౡ

I shall call myself Trudeth. When my father dies, I will bury him in the back-yard near the old dog, Gyro, by the fence lined with bloodred hollyhocks. If I move from the house, I will dig him up. I will wrap the box in heavy quilts. He must go where I go, where Trudeth goes, because we are bound with heavy twine.

I cut my hair like his, swept the sides back slick. I took his Levis and his shirts.

Trudeth.

Trudeth Clark.

He gave me cowboy boots and sent me to college. He never wrote letters. He did not have to.

I knew.

There were just the two of us.

He wanted a boy. He wanted a lawyer, a judge.

"Where are you going, Lucy?"

"To the Bar."

"Where are you going now, Trudeth?"

"To the Bar."

"Why Trudeth Clark, Lucy?"

"Because there is no judgment."

"Who are you Trudeth?"

"Not a metaphor."

&

I shall have to put the horse down someday soon. In Texas they take the meat and send it to France or Japan. The horse's eye watches me when I come to the fence. It is the biggest eye that I know, set in a glass socket. Old eunuch of a horse. Slow man. Hoof heavy. I have watched the death of horses at the vet school. I have seen the fetal pigs in brine in glasses on the shelf.

❧

Here is something that makes me laugh: the Carpenter Brothers out by Hayden.

They ordered brides by mail, girls sent from the East in 1911. They sat at their table and picked out their mates. They met the train at the Steamboat Depot on Friday, married them on Saturday.

Then, for years, they drove into town to get the mail shipments. They loaded their old 1927 truck each Wednesday.

The Carpenter boys had rich relatives back East who sent the brothers boxes and boxes of things that civilized people might need. One box was filled with glass doorknobs that cut the light into patterns on their shirts when they held them to the light. The doorknobs arrived in winter. The colors played on the snow outside the barn. The brothers laughed at the ornaments, saw their breath freeze in white mist.

I'm told the brothers took the box inside till spring. They had no need for glass knobs. But, then, in May, they took it out.

One of them found two old belts and hooked them into one long. The other gathered four of the glass doorknobs together tying them with fishing line like a bunch of carrots.

They walked out to the meadow where they kept the old, castrated bull who spent his time sleeping, opening one eye only when he had to.

Flies teased his head. His flesh was warm in the May sun.

Over the fence the brothers could see the cows with their calves, munching on the grass, standing in lady-like groups. Separated in another pasture, the fertile bulls stood, dull-brained.

The brothers approached the old bull, one bent down and spoke to him, gentled him. The other brother reached and slipped the belt under his hind quarters. They coaxed the bull to stand then, offering a handful of hay, and when he did, the brother was able to sling the other part of the belt around the haunches and hook it, and there under the bull's belly hung the four glass knobs, breaking the light into patterns, clinking together in a deep fine-glass tone.

The brothers watched.

The bull looked back at his hind end, heard something, must have felt the weight. As he walked, he had no way of knowing that diamond glass had replaced his lost testicles. He moved to the fence to let the women see.

The brothers laughed till their eyes watered.

The bull turned at the sound. His eye was glassy.

Here is what makes me cry: I saw the black dog, dead on the road. I saw the brown and white dog, the spotty one, dead by the park. I saw the golden one, dead by the mining museum.

Trudeth will bury you, I told each one.

And Trudeth did.

EVEN THE STONES

1.

He phoned me. He said his fingernails were turning blue. He said that was a sign.

Looking out the window at the drift of snow, the clumps of cold, I told him I would come. He always taught me that something has to measure.

2.

The man next door is called Terry. He is a real estate agent. Every Sunday he goes to the hospice, called St. John's, and assists the dying in taking their breakfast. Terry sells houses and he plants flowers, but he tells me it's all tissue. In feeding the dying their scrambled eggs, lifting the cup of coffee to their tongues, looking in their eyes, Terry says, there are interstices. One afternoon he looked up at me from his flower bed when I asked and said, "When it's time, take your father to St. John's. All is water."

Greek Orthodox monks run St. John's. They wear black cassocks and stovepipe hats. Their faces extend in long beards. At the hospice, there is a small room, a chapel with golden, Byzantine paintings of the Virgin and her Son. Their faces have dark eyes. Their gowns just simple rows of lines, waves of flatness. Even at night the room glows. There are three candles, and if you are quiet, the flickering makes the Virgin nod.

3.

I have a tinted photograph of my father, thin in his World War II military uniform, his face angular, my mother posed beside him, looking like the young Judy Garland, her brown hair pulled back from her face. She is wearing a green suit with round buttons. Face to face, pressed together there they assume a life after the War. He has defined it, calculated two children. On an engineer's salary that is what he can afford. She has agreed. I see them sitting in his car by the lake at City Park. He is telling her that he has estimated that they could live in the south part of Denver and that her mother, soon to be his mother-in-law, will help her with the children, a boy and girl. Yes, she is saying, such passion in one sound. Yes. He is telling her that he will be back from the war by the last weeks of 1945. She is nodding. He wants to know if they should marry now, if it would be fair to her. Now, she says, now, and she smiles like Judy Garland.

4.

One of the monks takes me to the admissions office. There are papers to be signed. This monk, called Frederick, tells me that they can make him comfortable. That is what they can do. They can take the fear away, and my father will breathe better. Right now, he says, your father fears breathing. I nod. Frederick says he will assign him a room with a bed by the window. I follow the wheelchair. I sit beside his bed. We can see two fruit trees, barren now, and a feeder with seeds for a squirrel who comes each morning and hangs upside down off the yellow plastic top to retrieve his food. I bring a plant, a red flower against the green walls, and together we watch the snow as it touches a picnic table and a wooden fence and a cement statue of a deer, some wild spirit caught in a body that holds it to the ground. My father asks the cost of squirrel seed. He is calculating the volume in the feeder against the cost of sunflower seeds and grain.

I suppose I have spent my life trying to prove him wrong about all this calculation. I can hear my mother telling me that she loved him at first sight. She told my grandmother she would marry him the next day, should he ask. As I grew up, learning to use his slide rule to do math, watching his head bent over my chemistry equations, delighting in helping me see salt, I could feel his brain somehow, if that is possible. I could feel the pressure of his order. He sliced his birthday cake in perfect fractions of $1/16^{th}$ or $1/12^{th}$. He opened gifts slowly, removing the paper with his pocketknife, folding the paper in perfect squares to be saved and used again. It all measures, he would say.

He was a metallurgist and he could read the nature of stones. I would find them by the river as he fished in his long rubber waders, wearing his fishing vest spotted with hooks, pockets filled with line. I would watch his line go out and tap the water, tap the quiet space by the rocks, the still place where the rainbow trout hid. I would watch him finesse the fish to his will, bringing it out like a lyrical dance of motion. And he would put it in a basket hung on a leather strap around his neck. As he left the river, I would be there with my stones. Sedimentary, he would say. Igneous. Metamorphic. Biblical words, for me. Sedimentary with traces of Igneous. Pure Metamorphic. Analysis of Matter. Naming the world:

Brown.

Rainbow.

Cutthroat.

5.

Terry next door is a quiet man. He gardens in the spring and his tomato plants burst in August in the sun. We talk over the fence. He tells me that he is putting in Canterbury bells, these fluted British flowers from a package that a friend sent him from overseas. He has a cat named Ivan who is fearless, a prowling cat who sings to the female cat down the street, sitting on the porch of that house in the early morning, howling. I like to watch Ivan strut. He will look over at me with his yellow eyes just to be certain I am seeing him, strutting down the path at the side of the house, his tail making slices of the air.

6.

When the nurse leaves the room, my father shows me the blue of his fingernails. Blue moons, he makes a joke, and he looks at me with a crooked smile, his eyes asking if I could please just stop what is happening. I take his hand. It is warm. He says he wants to go to the dining room to have his supper. They have tables there with white tablecloths, he says, and he has made a reservation. They only charge $4.00 for a guest. He says the menu is chicken pot pie and peas and chocolate pudding. I help him from the bed and into his chair. As we move slowly down the hall to the cafeteria, he waves at a man who is watching the news on television, at a nurse who, he says, is called Besty, and at a woman in her 90s, white haired, her face painted with white powder, her lips bright red and shaped in a Kewpie doll pout, propped up against the pillows wearing a blue robe. Last night, he tells me, gesturing for me to lean close so he can whisper, she came to his room and stood in the doorway and said his name and she had nothing on. He chuckles with the wonder of it, "She had nothing on."

It is a quiet place, this hospice. They sit and read or sleep. They wait. The squirrel eats his breakfast, then his lunch, then his dinner. The tree boughs outside the window sigh even with the weight of the blue jay. If you go down the hall, they do not turn to look at you. They are encased in a knowing that you do not understand. They sit and read or sleep. Sometimes they watch the artist man on the television at 3 o'clock. He makes the canvas white with gesso paint and scrubs it over in blue. He makes mountains in purple and pine trees with long skirts. He puts a deer in the corner with a rack of antlers. He says that the tree is happy. Those who are watching smile because they are not afraid of breathing. Sometimes they point when the painter surprises them, placing a fish in the stream, a rainbow trout with spots and a blush of dawn on its sides.

7.

At my mother's funeral years ago, when everyone had gone, I stood and looked at her in her best red dress. I had placed black beads around her neck. She was doll-like, and I bent to kiss her, to make a promise I will never tell, and my lips touched the cold cheek, the cold August air, and I can still feel the cold and artificial touch, the doughy nothingness that she was now, but I promised anyway. Then, later, when I went to the Tarot reader, a fragile soul named Bonnie with a big white cat, I sat in her living room at her table spread with black velvet cloth. Bonnie placed my cards on the table. She said my mother had gone long ago. She was not lingering or hovering. She put another card down on the velvet. There, she said, there on your shoulder is your father.

8.

If the flowers are transient things, I ask Terry, why do you put them in the ground every year?

They are transient things.

If Ivan is ephemeral, why do you feed him?

He is ephemeral.

And when we die where do we go?

Where the black crows go.

Where is that?

Ask them.

My kitchen window faces the side of Terry's house. I can see the ladies he brings home. Pretty ones he meets as he tries to find them houses. Selling Real Estate is a seductive thing. He must describe the house in terms that chime. He must represent the Romance of the World in a two-bedroom apartment with a pool. I have sent friends to Terry and he has found them studio apartments in the inner city where they can walk to work in places that other realtors would never think to look, bohemian places with balconies that face the river, dark and secluded condominiums that overlook the town, small white boxes where windows open onto towers of light and, looking down, you can trace the patterns of the lovers in the horse drawn carts. His secret is that he compares the place to Dublin where his grandfather lived. He can speak with a bit of a brogue, and he tells people looking for houses that he is the seventh son of a seventh son and that the stones wept at his grandmother's funeral. Even the stones wept. Even the stones. On the weekends the ladies come at night and leave early on Sunday because, as he explains to them, Terry has to feed the dying.

9.

When I was seven, I collected pennies. Most were coppery, shiny. Some were black or grey, and I put them in a mayonnaise jar on my dresser. If I found one in the halls at school, I made a wish and brought it home. At night I asked my mother to check her change purse to see if she had one, and I would put it with the others, listening to the sound of the single coin deepen as the jar filled. My friend, Diane, said it was bad luck to pick up one if it was face down, that probably someone had licked it and put it there.

I did not believe that. I thought that, somehow, it was waiting for me, that somebody, my grandfather maybe, had dropped it from the sky. He used to call me his Copper Penny, I tell Diane, because of my hair. He painted houses and wore white overalls. When he came home, he smelled of turpentine. There was paint on the rims of his glasses, and his hands were like a speckled trout.

10.

And do we come to exist in the trees?

Some.

In the water?

All is water.

In the spider web beside the peonies?

All is tissue.

In the moth.

Yes.

11.

My father was an engineer. He built roads and we went with him every summer. He had to estimate it all, yards of dirt, equipment, mileage, dynamite to open the mountain. He had to call in front-end loaders and graders to shape mountains, to make order. He had large leather boots that were thick with red dirt and a slide rule and a pocket full of pencils. He drove the rutted roads like they were flat, stopped beside a stream and reached a tin cup in and drank the mountain water, cold, cold, cold. He stood quietly when he saw a frightened deer, watching us watch it, found the best motel with knotty pine siding and a swing set, but no pool, and fixed us peanut butter and jelly which we ate as we walked around the blocks of the town or sat on the courthouse lawn while envelopes were opened at the Bid meeting, and we could tell as he came toward us what the year would be like, if the road would be his or if it would belong to the man from Pueblo who had extra rigs and cut costs to the point of danger.

12.

And is the soul a fish?

That, too.

Swimming in the reeds at the dark bottom?

Sometimes.

Coming to the top in a rush if someone drops food on the surface?

Perhaps.

Does it know time?

That's unimportant.

And, in the winter, does it have breath below the ice?

Breath always.

Does it turn blue at the end?

I do not know there is an end.

13.

One Sunday when I was eleven, my father took all the pennies from the jar I kept. He won them from me, turning cards over on the floor of the living room, showing me how to count to "21" or to duck under. He had come up with a system. He wanted to see if it worked. I listened to the language. Hit Me. I Fold. And it was so dark, so painful to the skin. The jar empty then, he told me to get ready to go to church. He would drop me at the door. Things have to measure, he said.

Nothing in the world is free, my father told me.

The sun is free.

No, he told me, it takes money to live to see it.

The purple mountains and the birds are free.

No, he told me, it takes money to live to see it.

The air is free.

No, he made certain I understood, it takes money to breathe.

14.

I sit with my father in the white hospice room. Bob Ross, the painter, is on television. We are watching together. It is three o'clock in the afternoon, early April. He will die next Tuesday, but for now he is complete. He watches Bob Ross make happy trees and mountains of snow. He sees the evergreen trees become forest. He smiles at the large buck with the antlers Ross puts in the corner.

He is counting the points on the antlers to find the age of the deer.

He does not look anywhere but at the paint. He is still calculating time and growth potential. He is breathing evenly. But I look at his face and his skin is thin, onion skin, lightly mottled with age spots, his blue eyes faded, squinting. He is concentrating on the paintbrush, on the process of transfiguration, watching wet pigment become solid stone, trees rising in impasto paint, and mountains made of blue acrylic in the distance.

I want to tell him that even the stones weep. I do not.

The night my father will die, next Tuesday, I will stand at the bed. He will have talked to me all day, asking me to open a door or a gate. He will botch up words, and I will struggle to understand and to bring him soup or chocolate pudding. He will push it aside. The hospice will put him on a "Watch."

He will say that he sees his fingernails are turning blue. He will laugh sometimes at things he sees. The cart will come down the hall. A man will give
me a glass of orange juice as I stand watch. I will tell my father that I loved
the kite he made from newspaper and string. I will recall to him how he
engineered it, cutting it out, a large pentagon, and how he folded the paper
and glued the corners. I will ask him if he remembers how he cut up my old
undershirts to make the tail or how when he lifted it to the wind, the sun
darkened and the kite ascended with a chain link of cloth tied like a sentence
dropping to me from the sky.

STILL

֍

Somewhere on the east side of New Mexico, they tell me, she sat still.

֍

Because the woman eats apples with mayonnaise, dipping them in the white pudding.

Because history is that tin type, the young Englishman with a wife and baby on a beach somewhere. It is self-reflexive. It erases itself from the edges. The man wears a dark coat and bowler hat. She is pulling away, holding the white bundle and letting go. She is still innocent. She believes the baby will grow grey hair.

Because the woman eating apples is selling antique things, in the place on HWY 50. She has an old school chalkboard with a wooden frame. It is too tall, she says, to fit in anyone's house, unless you take the casters off, but, she will tell you as she dips the green apple in mayonnaise, you will ruin it if you take the casters off.

֍

The place called Wagon Mound is off 1-25, but was off the old New Mexico HWY 84, and before that was off a wagon trail to Santa Fe, and was, before that, off a crossroads where two roads met and someone put in a saloon hall. It is boarded up now. There is a wooden walkway, the grocery, the hotel with café, then a building marked POOL All of it boarded. Across the street a sort of storehouse with "A. Reynolds" on the sign at the top of the roof. No date.

Two dogs, one black, one brindle sit in the shade of the one cottonwood tree. They watch. They do not care that A.Reynolds had a storehouse or that one woman sat still in an upstairs room and looked at things out the window.

With civilization all boarded up, the land stretches wide there--one herd of black cattle, just scattered seeds, and sky, sky, sky with horsetail strips and, in the July rain, scuds that lurk. The wind blows sometimes, but there are spaces where nothing stops it, so you cannot see it.

The wind is just there, erasing what it wants to.

&

Long ago, she sat there and she died there, or somewhere nearby, Springer, maybe. No one speaks of it, her father so famous and infamous, they speak of him. He died in Boggsville in Colorado in an old grey house, his young wife, dead only months before, his heart arresting, his cough bringing up phlegm and the doctor sending him home by wagon, and the man dying, perhaps, in the wagon, the boards repeating a syllabic sound, something like *Adios*. The hero man, the dime novel frontiersman, passing into language so they can read of him, or speak.

He had friends in Boggsville, in Bent's Fort. Probably, in some novel, though, he stopped at Wagon Mound for a drink on the porch. He may have seen a brindle dog.

Because he is a narrative. Because I choose to put him there, sipping whiskey and thinking of his young wife, of the piece of silk, pink with small roses, he will take home to her in Taos, his reunion gift, something pretty, a trinket to pay for lovemaking.

Because she is his third wife, young and beautiful.

Because she will die of her child-birthing.

Because he loved the first wife best.

&

Perhaps she, the child they named Rebecca, had her famous father's wide brow and the pinched cheeks. Perhaps she had his mind, his depression. He was a sad man. You can see in the black and white photographs that, though the skin ages, the eyes stay white. Though he is dead, he continues to read the text of the world.

Perhaps Rebecca had her mother's eyes. There are not many pictures of the mother, only that young one when she was 14 or 16, no more. Her hair is pulled back, and her dark eyes make questions for you.

She does not know that one winter day she will watch the Governor of her New Mexico village die, that she, standing with her cousin at a small window, her cousin, the wife of the Governor, will see the Governor scalped in front of the adobe house, and she, with her older cousin, will take silver spoons from the trunk and dig through the adobe wall, scraping old mud and straw, digging to make a hole in the house, at the back, where the Indians, come to attack, cannot see them, digging quietly, hearing the sound of spoon against earth, hearing the screaming and the war sounds, watching the dog run in circles, and she will hear the sound of gurgling, perhaps from the cousin's children clawing at the hole, perhaps from the dog who ran after its tail, perhaps from her own throat.

ဆာ

Because we leave ourselves to interpreters.

Because when we never tell them, they can never really know.

Because we become traces.

Because interpreters interpret anyway.

ဆာ

Ft. Garland is a military fort. Her father commanded it, some time before he died. This daughter Rebecca would have been four years old, then there would have been another child, and then, finally, a sister, who would come to life in two years, 1868, the one who would kill the mother in the childbed. In a matter of weeks after the death-in-birth, that same year, 1868, her father would die in a wagon, perhaps, in a house, only weeks after his wife. And, this girl, Rebecca, on the list of children's names, 1863-1884, would be an orphan before she had memory of what that word meant. I theorize this 4 year-old child, called Rebecca, born 1863, was the difficult one.

Named after her grandmother, she probably rode bareback at an early age. She probably reached up and cut her hair off in swatches, ragged endings, poetic retribution. She probably smoked an uncle's clay pipe. Something or another she wanted denied her, she howled at the world. She could have been manly, like her father, a muscular piece of flesh that challenged reason. She might have been delicate and fluid as silk like her mother, never one to announce herself, pensive, perhaps, and full of black bile. But the physical body is only the vessel. She was, I say, false as water.

Observing her youngest sister, the sister who killed her mother coming into this world, may have taught Rebecca, the older one, this lesson: Women must kill their mothers to announce their own identity. Holding her mother's cold hand at the bed, her newborn sister, called Josephine, yelling her lungs off in the other room, the one called Rebecca most likely felt her mother to be a wooden santos figure, an Angel. Holding her mother's hand each day for the several weeks as the woman whimpered in her deathbed bed, Rebecca must have concluded that this thing, called Josephine after their mother's mother, this sister-baby-child, would come to know the condition of the wandering female pilgrim. Rebecca would teach her.

We cry, Rebecca might have thought, that we are come here. But, then, as the fates would have it, Josephine would grow to wander longer, would live in Boggs and in Raton, would live, probably, in Springer, but not in Wagon Mound. And when this baby sister child, called Josephine, then called Josie, who killed her mother being born, finally died, last daughter of the Scout, no one knew it. The New York papers ran 110 words about her life. In capital letters the headline said: Kit Carson's Daughter Dead.

In the Eastern paper, one short paragraph about this Josephine, this daughter of the noted "Scout and Indian fighter," a record of how she was admitted to the Territorial Insane Asylum in East Las Vegas, New Mexico, in 1898, where, it says, she fell terribly ill and died there in June 1902. The report does not mention her painted face, her wool skirt, her wandering the streets of Raton wrapped in some old Spanish shawl.

She may have been tubercular, may have contracted diseases from the drovers at the bar. She may have been pock-marked with some scarlet disease.

Anyway, her sister Rebecca was long gone.

&

Consider this: when she was little, the Rebecca girl, born in 1863, learned to make preserves, to put by jelly. She stirred it in the pot. Her relative added sugar. They made concord grape. They made strawberry. Sometimes the woman relative, for whom she had no affection, made bread in the early morning, the loaves brown and sometimes burned, the jelly thick out of the jars. The girl Rebecca watched the relative eat a bite of bread and then dot her mouth with a cloth napkin. The relative said to always use cloth napkins. The girl, though, preferred to pick up the bread slice and, holding it over her head, pinching the edge as the jelly began to slide, glide it out of the bread held perpendicular to the ground, slide the jelly into her mouth like a slab of stone come out of the sky. She liked the feel of having too much at one time.

And at fifteen, I surmise, Rebecca must have heard word of the other girl, the one stolen by Indians in the mountains in Colorado. That girl had the same name as her sister, Josephine, called Josie. She, called Rebecca, must have known because troops were sent from Ft. Garland, black soldiers, Buffalo soldiers, sent to get that girl back. The point here is that someone said the syllables about the stolen women, about "mayhem"—an ever so substantial word, about the stingy man who was the Government Agent and the abduction and the outrage--all words that stayed alive.

Sitting on the porch with the relative, watching the grasses blow in the wind in Boggsville, her hair cut by her own hand into slices, all swathes of angles, the bangs on her forehead one inch long, she must have watched the horses and on that October afternoon, the news having reached her, she must have considered the death of the Government Indian Agent, the barrel stave rammed through his chest at the Indian Agency in Meeker, must have considered the other Josephine, called Josie. She must have imagined the raid on the Agency, an office that was meant to hand out blankets for the winter, a square fort. She knew military forts. That is what she knew. She imagined it in color. She saw the girl, the other Josephine, with long yellow hair and a straw hat, conventional kind of girl, baker of bread, student of cloth napkins.

She might have made up the story to tell her younger sister, the last child, called Josephine, to use this event as some sort of parable about rites of women, to get out the chalk and the board and draw the other Josephine and the Indian who grabbed her and swung her up on his horse and the one who grabbed that other Josephine's aging mother. She would move the chalk slowly, drawing in the raid and the trek across the hills, and the nights spent on the ground without fire, warm September nights, the horses tethered to trees. The questions were all about "outrage." Had the Indians "outraged" the women. The military would take down the report. A young Captain, who would wear the same cloth coat she vaguely remembered her father wearing, would, she knew, investigate.

She would draw the women in chairs, the Captain in a desk like the one her father used at Ft. Garland. She was not surprised when she heard that the women, when they were rescued, would not admit to the "outrage." They were mute.

I theorize that she liked that.

I say she always preferred the recalcitrant gesture if she could not have the howling one.

಄

Rebecca knows the colcha embroidery. It is a thick and overlapping process. The needle has a large eye. The wool strands are bright of color. The pattern simple: a blue horse, a green bird, a spindly flower with a giant yellow bloom. Women lose their eyesight over the work. The tighter the better. The circle of ponies, the eruption of vines. Rebecca knows it can take your eyes.

Where did you get that piece? Josephine asks her sister Rebecca.

What?

The shawl. The red shawl with the flowers.

A man.

What man?

The dark-haired man.

He gave it to you?

Yes. He said he bought it in Texas, a Mexican shawl, colcha.

Why did he give it to you?

Because.

಄

Rebecca married at Ft. Garland. That much is true.

She wore a blue dress made by the relative and held, with the wildflower

82

bouquet of delphiniums and vines, a cloth handkerchief, the relative's idea. I invent here. That people said she looked like her mother. I can only surmise. That the Commandant performed the civil ceremony in the room where her father used to be the Commandant, I say, but know not. That she said the vows. That she signed the paper. That no one remembers the groom's name.

That people said, It is Kit's daughter, I can guarantee.

That she coughed as she left the Fort with the groom. That it was summer. That the winged grasshoppers made a chirping sound. That the air was still, no dust. That part is standard.

That she loved the man or that she had a powerful disregard, I say, but I know not.

No, I say, because.

Because it was time.

Because she was ripe.

Because she knew already.

∞

The relative saw it many times, Rebecca's hateful eye, the disdain of her profile, the stomping to the front porch, the scissors taken to the hair, cutting it, cutting it, cutting it until her head was a feathered chicken skull and she stood there, her feet covered in black silk skeins of hair, in handful grabs of self. The last child, the sister Josephine, knew the older sister's temper. She felt the bites taken at her arm. She knew why the yellow dog, tail between its legs, moved away from Rebecca.

The relative said it was the abandonment, well, think of it, the relative said, to lose two parents in one season.

The relative talked to the priest in Boggsville. He said the Lord would fix it, that the Lord has his plans for Rebecca. The relative waited and watched for what the Lord would do. The relative ironed linen napkins, the remnant of family fortune, and folded them and put them in the drawer. The relative milked the cows. The relative cooked the stews and made the bread. One day, outside the window, after Rebecca's hair had grown back but her scowl still evident, the relative watched as a young man rode his horse up the road to the house. He was not an attractive man. His jaw was prominent and long. His hair was thin. He seemed awkward even when he breathed, and the sun had blotched his face in island spots. The second time he visited, the relative had to ask his name. It was, the relative thought, forgettable.

෪

The point is we do try to keep things. We make translations. We make things into words or we keep things in boxes. We take photographs. Something in us preserves.

I know a man who lived to be 94. A stubborn man. He did not want to leave anything out. He thought you could keep it all—in a box on the shelf. Like jam. Like that. The obituary says he was a photographer who thought it best to make photographs every day. He tried to frame every tree in the park, record every swan, see the way the paddles of the canoes made the mirror water take action. The Christmas trees are there, the same position every year, only the draperies change and the color of the room and the generations of dogs forced to sit by the gifts. And he stored everything in boxes in the basement. He had stereo shots and super 8. He had a Polaroid and, then, disposable cameras. The children used to crowd around him as he pulled the negative back to display their Polaroid selves standing next to the collie dog near the roses. The man never stopped capturing what reality he felt for, that he insisted be kept. The man had his method. History was product. He pointed the camera at everything he could see. He preserved it all.

Everyone agreed he was an annoyance.

I do not.

I prefer the cluttered mind.

෪

There are people who know how to write things down. They study plight, bad choices. They see that some things hold still and others whirl. They see that no one listens and we endanger birds.

Here's a story I think about: once I read a novel about a woman in the East, a grand sort of society woman who loses everything, a woman who is beautiful and wears silks and plumed hats, but a woman who finds her rich man gets tired of her. It all happens at the turn of the century. This woman, I can't remember the name, leaves her big mansion and finds humble housing in a rundown flat. To feed herself she makes hats with feathers, those hats she used to wear, hats that caused exotic birds to die, that caused hunters to raid islands and steal, that caused the poisoning of birds, the plucking of long plumes, the transport of feathers and birds to places like Cincinnati, to factories or small shops where women sat at tables, signs on the door, Charlotte's Millinery, places where the women stitched until their fingers bled, making chapeaux, turning women to hens. In the novel, the fallen woman lives in a small room and walks to the shop, snow falling, thin soles on her shoes, and she works with silk and feather. She pleats black satin, her eyes bent to the black thread moving in blackness and attaching the black jewel ornament, a bauble like a bird's eye next to a stem of feather.

In the end she drinks morphine in hot tea, and she dies there in the room with feathers.

But then that is an interpretation. It may, you know, have been an accident.

&

Let's agree, then, that the Lewises lived for a while in Alamosa, these newlyweds, this couple, Rebecca and the forgettable man last name of Lewis.

Let's say that at first Rebecca tried to be like her domesticated relative. She tried to make bread. She tried to smile at the lady next door when the lady was in her tomato patch. She tried to make do, to let go the desire to be elsewhere. She dressed each day and pinned up her hair. She walked to town to buy cloth and tinned things. Remembering her mother and the childbed, though, she turned away from him in bed, refusing the boy, denying him. Let the girl over the mountains be outraged. Let that girl die in childbed and become a santos figure.

And the cough got deeper, the hoarseness longer, and the fevers came, fevers that brought on chills, chills that translated to fevers. She gasped with the dust of the street. She covered her mouth with the handkerchiefs the relative had given her, white linen with tatting on the edge. She heated water on the stove and held a towel over her head, and bending over the pot, took in great draughts of steam, trying to settle the disruption inside. At night she wheezed, breathing and then echoing that breath like something was talking back to her. She left the bed. In the pantry, she found the bottle and gulped the whiskey she kept in the cupboard, saving it for cakes. And the whiskey was like sweet jarred-honey down her throat.

Then, one day, when he had gone out somewhere to some duty he felt, she dressed herself, bundled herself, layered on the winter skirts, stuffed nightwear in a pouch, found her one ornament, the shawl and the glass bottle. Her head was thick with something. Her forehead was hot to her touch. And she walked out the door to leave the town, and she sat in the stagecoach and watched the place rattle away and, she could not help herself, as the coach moved beyond Alamosa and past Ft. Garland, and she thought, for a moment, she thought she saw her father there, only her father as he was long ago, his blue uniform, the man of order, and the new Commandant and, then, as the coach rattled on again, she thought for a moment of the wedding, the promise she made that day a year ago to the odd boy whose name she, too, refused to remember. She watched the hills of La Veta and the turn on the dust road down toward Raton and then to Springer or was it, perhaps, Wagon Mound? Then she slept in the horse coach as it moved and shifted. When it stopped, there, she got out. She coughed her way to a hotel. It was a small and open town. It might have been Wagon Mound.

෪

We leave it to interpretation, to nuance.

The father became a hero of the West, became words.

One written record has a Rebecca married to a Lewis, John. It says Rebecca was born in 1864, not 1863, in April, and Rebecca died in 1885, not 1864m in April. She is four days short of being 21 years. The list says she gulped, yes, it says "gulped" morphine. The list says "suicide" for Rebecca.

When I look for the younger, the last, sister, Josephine, on the family lists, all is chaos. She married someone called Squires and the list says she died in 1892 or else, as the list also reports, she married a second time, someone called Howard, and died in 1902. One obituary list says Josephine died in an asylum in Las Vegas, New Mexico. Another says Josephine went mad. No matter. Something happened. As for me, I can see Josephine dancing. If I close my eyes, she is dancing in a red Mexican shawl. She is whirling and whirling and whirling in a thick wool shawl with loops of embroidery. In my mind Josephine would not even have tried to make bread or iron napkins. She would have not noticed the spindly lady who lived next door who worked in the tomato patch. Josephine had no time to notice or to sit still. She preferred whirling.

I say the Carson women, Rebecca and Josephine, had just enough cold in their veins to want it their way. Rebecca had a philosophical meanness. The world was a hard shell. Josephine saw tinsel everywhere. She ran to tinsel, to shiny things, but only when she paused in her whirling.

I will allow this, though, with Rebecca gone, I can see Josephine gone to find her. Rebecca is 20 when she disappears and Josephine is 15, and Josephine might choose to go to look for the runaway, to look for a sister, even one who bites. Well, really, it is the most Josephine could do for anyone, for a sister, for example, what we do when we take time to sit at a table to talk to the runaway or when we sit at the bedside and watch a runaway who is dying, when we know the runaway chose to take the morphine, chose it, and we sit and watch things happen and memorize them so that we can translate them into words and images and make the runaway breathe again.

So, Rebecca, wearing all of her four skirts at once, in layers, her hair tucked up in a black cloth hat, her pocketbook filled with a few things she needs, one small bottle, in particular, has come to Springer by herself. It is March and cold, yet there is dust. Rebecca is coughing dust. And, yes, Josephine has come from Boggsville. Better always to come *from* Boggsville. Josephine finds Rebecca in the one rooming house, in a rented room. Rebecca is on the bed. She is frayed. She is still. She watches the ceiling. Josephine, for as long as she can concentrate, sits at the bedside watching her sister fray. In Springer, Josephine pats her sister's hand.

I am being eaten up, Rebecca is saying. I am being outraged. I am walking away.

You are.

Even our mother lived longer.

She did.

I know that she will not be waiting.

She will not.

I know the next place is a space like this, wide and windy.

Yes.

It is all sage and sky.

Yes.

And, while they won't remember, they will be haunted.

They?

We will be on a list.

List?

Because a beet in the ground, Rebecca says, a sugar beet mis-planted. . . it turns.

Yes.

When it is planted the wrong way. . .it twists itself.

Yes.

And the consequences of a silence is a turning. . .

Yes.

Josephine gets up. She moves to the window. She can see the barn that says "A. Reynolds."
Josephine is patting her skirt, stretching her shoulders. Perhaps her back is tight. On the chair opposite her in the room, there, draped over the spindle back, is something she likes, her sister's red shawl, a lazy shawl with silk fringe aflame in the light.

Absent thee, Rebecca is talking to the molded tin forms on the ceiling.
Erase the left side, Rebecca is saying to the forms, . . .and move to the right until you must sit down, legless.
Josephine releases her sister's hand. She is standing now, moving to the chair, pulling the shawl from the chair back and moving it in a slow circle up to her shoulders, wrapping herself in embroidery and silk.
Josephine is at the window. She is looking down. A man in a dark vest, tidy man with a bowler hat is moving across the street. She concentrates on him. His name is Squires.

Absent thee, Rebecca is talking again.
Josephine is humming. She looks down to see the man look up. The man, she knows, cannot see the one they call Rebecca who is erasing herself. The man is looking up and, she knows, he cannot absent himself. He can only see Josephine, framed in the upstairs window, shrouded in red, doing, as he will learn, what she does best, dislodging herself from mortal responsibility,

looking and wanting.

Save the eyes till last, Rebecca is still talking to herself, so they can assess the consequences of the world without you.

Josephine does not turn to see her sister is white as alabaster, a santos figure now. Josephine is humming. She is moving and the fringe on the shawl, the satin ribbons, are making the quiet sound of stream water. Josephine is swaying now. For a moment she thinks of the relative who told her to sit still, told her to sit and see. Josephine remembers that Rebecca could sit still, but Rebecca is always wanting to erase herself. No, Josephine is not one to sit still. Josephine, she tells herself, Josephine must whirl.

ஐ

Because someone wrote a letter to the relative.

Because, probably, it was Josephine.

Because, in blocked-out and penciled writing, someone wrote short words, Rebecca gulped morphine.

Rebecca died April 9, 1884.

Because, getting up from the table, placing the ironed napkin at her place, the relative moved to the Bible and wrote in Rebecca's name and death date.

Because we all pass into words and some get more words than others.

Because someone made a list.

Because the consequence of a silence is a turning.

II.

And I have sometimes seen in my mind, soon after I have seen in my mind the things just mentioned, one or another detail of a place in my mind where I see together things that I might have expected to lie forever far apart. . . .

—Gerald Murnane, "Invisible Yet Enduring Lilacs"

Still, I must not forget that I once managed to put these things into writing.

—Maurice Blanchot

THE SEA POTATO

You make a loop and pull another through and make a chain and the hand works like a sort of bird or like a red crane standing on one needle leg in a pond taking water, and you can go there to the shop with the yardgoods and the buttons and the oil cloth and the antique sugar bowls and some old pitchers with strange brown birds with grand eyes and small heads printed on white porcelain, birds with large bird feet, and the morning of that other day, I found the picture of a withered thing, a picture of a round and stitched thing that came from down in the sea in a burrow of sand and mud, a mucus covered thing, but that was then, this other day, and on this day I only saw the yarn through the window, the thread that makes the loops that you pull other loops through, and the shop was called the Fringe, something about edgings, if I remember, and I went in because she talks to me in thread loops, in old things, like a mystery of other, like when the fisherman brought it up from the sea and spoke, holding the odd thing with hairy spines, like threads, is how he said it, and I was thinking of the brown bird with the long legs and he said, sea potato, but that was online and soundless, just the word and a digital picture, and he said it was a vegetable come from the sea, sea potato, the fisherman said again, and there was a hole for excess, for food, he said, and, he said, for breath, that maybe the vegetable, the sea potato, could breathe, but then the shop lady said, see the grey stone on the counter, a river stone, she said, see how it is covered in thread crochet, brown like the birds on porcelain, because it was a magic stone, and she sent me to the back of the Fringe to meet the small woman with the black eyes who was cutting cloth, brown paper patterns lining the yardgoods on the table, patterns held to the cloth by stones, and the dark-eyed woman smiled and said, yes, she made it, she made the crochet on the stone, and I asked if the stone was magic, and she smiled and said it was a grateful stone, and you should hold it in your hand, she said, and think of what you are grateful for, sit still, she said, and think, and the expert, that other day, online, said this was not a sea potato, no, not a sea potato, not a root vegetable, no, it was an urchin, one that could breathe in water, and the spiny threads were spines that float, and her hands, if you could watch her hands, made loops of thread, and long ago spoke in thread, and now that stone was speaking to me, its loops held still, patterned loops, telling me to take it to the river and put it where the rocks were wet, just there, down F street, past the Fringe and yardgoods and buttons, to the water in the river, and saying to put it there, by the river rocks where the sound of roiling water made music like the first music on the earth, and, yes, it was saying, yes, to put it there where the river makes whirls and where the plashing of the water will rain on it and where it will breathe and its spiny parts sprout and loop and loop and loop.

THE CENTER

1.

Donna told me how to do it. She said to get eight stones from the river. She said to dry them and to put them on my table and to sit and look at them. She said to take time with each one, to pick it up, to find the starcharts. Then she said, once that thinking was done, to paint them all blue and to start again. See them, Donna said, as other things, things that are not stones. Nothing, you see, is simply one thing. She said to put them on a shelf and leave them there to watch me.

2.

At school, I would ask the class to draw their family and their pets. They were young, and they would draw stick people, liney and stalwart replicas of family with a square, brown house or blue, tall mountains behind the people. Usually there would be a ragged, stick dog, a stick father and mother, several children, sometimes an old uncle in purple, faded and partially disappearing. Sometimes a stick cat with long stick whiskers.

I told them it was a rhetoric of sticks.

I saw that, invariably, the stick people all wore big round shoes on their feet, shoes that were mostly colored blue, and the stick pets had rounded feet as well, circles of paws or webbed feet at the end of stick legs.

They stood for the portrait with their feet heel to heel, the rounded toes of their two shoes pointing to opposite sides of the paper while a large, round orange sun with spikey stick rays generating from it, smiled from the sky.

3.

Donna is a home nurse who specializes in feet. She works on my odd left toe at the Community Center near my house. The doctor sent me to Donna at the Center because Donna is a traveling nurse and the toe on my left foot, the Great Left Toe, had been broken once and the toenail had begun to twist, to point left. It began to warp and flute and to become an arrow pointing left. Donna was one of two "toe nurses" at the Center. She would, the Insurance Company lady told me, fix it.

That day I sat there watching people, and mostly older people arrived every 15 minutes, their legs stiff, their canes tapping the floor, their movement stick-precise, each step mediated. The two nurses at the Center had these foot rests ready for you and you sat on orange plastic chairs. I say this because it wasn't like a fancy pedicure parlour. It was more like a community center where people played bridge or took piano lessons in the afternoon where the nurses took over a room twice a month in the morning. And if I were to describe the outside of the Center for you, I would say the Center is a small green box with large flowers outside, white flowers with reddish centers and petals that were the size of dinner plates, fragile, large-blossomed-plated flowers with stamen thick with yellow fuzz.

Donna is inside in the piano-toe-bridge game-conversation room. You would know Donna. You have seen Donna before though you have never seen her—the large woman in black stretch pants and a cotton shirt with short sleeves and flowers. She has short cropped hair, graying, and tennis shoes with thick soles and she looks over at you, tilting her head to see you over the rims of her rimless glasses. She asks for your insurance card. She says that, according to the records, you get four visits a year, January to January. If you want more, it is $35.00 per foot session, $15.00 for finger nail trims.

Donna wears a blue lanyard around her neck. She has a special name tag badge, if you look, and her lanyard has the words, "Faith, Hope, and Charity" in white print, and, I suspect, Donna got it from somewhere else. The other nurse has a plain black lanyard. And the other thing I always notice is Donna's gaze. When I look into Donna's eyes, I see her glasses with their thick glass lenses make Donna's eyes get bigger like insect eyes. The glasses are magnifiers, really, and Donna sees every detail. And Donna talks to me as she works on my foot.

4.

Once you know the blue stones are watching, Donna says, you need to start a second collection. You might find four pine cones or six brass bells or five

94

dimes. It is a collection, a cabinet of curiosities.

And each collection must be studied and each collection must be re-named, for, as Donna says, each collection is an intersection, as you will come to see.

5.

Sometimes at the Center, I look at the pictures on the wall, paintings that the neighborhood seniors have done in art class. There are dishes of pears and vases of roses, an aloe plant and a goldfish bowl. Still Life things. Tenderness and order. I look at them, mostly painted in thick impasto strokes, and then I take my Great pointy-arrow Toe into Donna. As if it is required, Donna always starts by explaining why she must begin her foot work by dragging a thin piece of wire over the top of the foot and then the bottom to see if I have feeling in the foot. The feelings in the foot can die, is the way Donna puts it. So, Donna says, I must check for feeling. Nerve endings die. Feet die. Then she puts my foot on her leg and she turns her back to me and I talk to her shoulder.

I have noticed that Donna starts with the good foot and invariably, I find, when Donna begins on the foot with the bad toe, the bent and twisted thing, trying to shape it, carve it into a workable part, well, usually, around that time, her patient Dorothy arrives, tapping her cane, wearing a sort of silky and fancy brown dress and sunglasses and calling out to Donna with the words, *I am here now, Donna!*, It seems Dorothy always shouts as she arrives, Dorothy with her face made up like Gloria Swanson, if you remember, in that movie, "Sunset Boulevard," where Gloria comes down the stairs, made-up, thick lipstick and eye blackening and says, *I am ready for my close up, Mr. DeMille*. Like that. Only Dorothy always shouts, *Donna, I am paying $20.00 an hour for my driver, so could you please hurry!* And Donna says, Have a seat, Dorothy. Have a seat.

6.

Once in my classroom, I had the students all draw a cup. I put the cup on a stool in the middle of the room and 37 of them drew it. Then I told them to get up and go around the room and see the cups on the drawings the other students made. One boy, I recall, years ago, went around and then came over to me. You know, he said, I don't think drawing a cup is about the cup.

No, I said, it is not.

7.

Donna told me, as she moved the thin wire over my right foot, that there is no death. Donna says the dead do not die. They are there at our shoulder. They sit at our feet. Donna says that when we remember, they breathe.

Then, as Donna is saying this, we both hear Dorothy, in the corner, tapping her stick.

Donna talks, and I can see Dorothy in her brown dress over Donna's shoulder, looking at her watch. Sometimes she raps her stick cane and, speaking to the air above her head, Dorothy remarks that time is money. Sometimes Donna, nodding at Dorothy, just continues and tells me about this old book she found that had a drawing of a centaur in it, an illustration of a myth, a picture of a man with a horse body. Donna said it was a good story where the centaurs helped the hero. She said that the drawing of this creature, part human and part horse, reminded her of this Marine Sergeant that she cares for who can only speak in lists of things to be done and who gives himself orders and who repeats them outloud as he sees them in his mind. She says he was in Vietnam and that he has a PTSD dog named Jake. Sometimes he asks her to fix Jake's nails when they come. Donna says that the dog Jake has a yellow PTSD service dog vest he wears. Donna says she doesn't mind. It only takes a minute and someone should tend to it. Jake lets her pick up his paws and looks into her eyes as she clips.

And somewhere over Donna's shoulder, we both hear Dorothy cough.

8.

A while ago I read about Days End Farm. The farm rescues horses. Days End searches certain farm buildings, they find sad and dying horses, on this day a full-sized stallion and a miniature stallion and a mare, emaciated creatures and standing in excrement in the darkness with old pigeons cooing and the barn saturated in the smell of disease and death. And there in the black frame was the picture of the white stallion with his boney sides and his long face and his rumpled grey mane and his sadness. If I show you the picture, you'll see that the horse is a white stick horse, his ribs showing and his hooves, never tended, never treated for years by a farrier. And you will see his four hooves and you will not want to look, but you will, and you will see that the hooves have grown and grown and have become long horns at the base of each leg, bone horns that twist and curl from the horse's hooves, growths of three-feet long extremities that funnel like long gourds on the ground, like fluted squash or ancient Asian slippers. Hard and continuous, each hoof grows round and round itself, it tunnels, so each foot is a bone-flute and the white stick horse cannot move. It can only stand and look back at you. It cannot walk. Its legs become grotesque ornaments and wooden shackles.

9.

I watch Donna, her thick arms holding my foot, her wide be-speckled face pressed down to see how the toenail is turning under itself. She has a concern for small things like a toenail. I often think that even when she was young, at the time when the eye doctor gave her the thick lenses, she somehow began to understand that the "self" and what comes out of the self must be measured by details, by looking back. I think she had a vision, not of centaurs, but of her own physical "self" as a sort of not-pretty and blind thing, an odd and growing image, a concept that she needed to pull off and let float away. I suspect the process hurt, that one day, looking through the glasses, I suspect it hurt to pull it off, the selfish and fungal part, and I suspect she stood there by a stick tree and watched it float away, like a kite, floating over the lake where a small fish jumped, and then she turned to tend to other things. I suspect she learned that we need to pay attention when something is going to hurt.

Donna says there is a fungus in a toenail. She says she knows my strange toe will soften and relax if, as she told me, I do not buy the $500 nail fungus ointments, but rather if I just to put Vicks Vapor rub on it. Just wipe it on, Donna says, and the nail will soften, the fungus will absorb the menthol.

10.

And in the article I was reading, it says the Days End people had to put one horse, the mare, down. They saved the white stick stallion and the small one, and the veterinarian and farrier sawed off the flutes of hooves that looked like something from a fantasy story, long wooden curls of something strange and prehistoric, something come out of the animal, something turning and turning and waiting to be tended.

11.

Now, watch. I am drawing a green box. I write CENTER on the door. Here I place some large white flowers and some big blue stones. And next I draw a stick figure with black stretch pants and a flowered blouse and thick glasses. I place her inside the box marked CENTER, smiling, but now, watch, I am drawing a copy of her stick self and this one is floating above the roof in the sky where I have drawn blue stars in patterns.

I draw myself sitting on an orange chair. I draw a brown dog beside me. I draw big, round blue feet for me and round blue paws for the dog. Again, I draw several small round and blue stones here and there. We are all watching and smiling.

At the bottom, in green and spindly letters, I begin a word. I write it in long-hand script, tall and fluid, wave-like. I inscribe the noun "INTERSECTION." As I finish the last "n," I draw the tail, the single line, back over the word and attach it to the "I" at the beginning. I make a frame, a crown, an elegance of space to contain the fluted quickening.

ON MERCURY

1.

As we grew up in this town, we were told that a man died in his house on Main Street. He was an old man from England who came to the town in the West to buy up land. He sat in his apartment and watched passersby through the curtains. His room was always dark. People said he was planning to buy up all of the town and plant cottonwood trees. He had decided to make a kingdom for himself, to colonize.

He planted the trees up and down the main roads. He did not do the work himself, but people said he purchased the trees and looked through his curtains to see if they would grow. This happened in 1929, and today the trees are tall. Long branches hold the blackbirds who turn their yellow eyes to watch us.

We were told that the man died in his apartment on Main Street. Someone killed him, sliced off his head, and locked him in the room with his dog. After a few days the dog began to howl, and when the police broke in, they found that the German shepherd had commenced to eat the man's flesh.

Our town myth was simple: a person could be eaten by his own dog.

2.

It was an odd choice to come to this town to make money. People told her that. We said that the only people who become rich in this town are the people who bring money with them to begin with and that, even then, those people lose some of it. But she was a large and jolly woman who seemed to trust something in the universe.

She collected thermometers. She wanted to open a thermometer store.

So she rented a shop on the plaza that had tried to be a morning coffee shop with doughnuts. She scrubbed the layers of doughnut pan grease from the walls. She swept up the sprinkles from under the counter edgings. She had workmen come in to take out the bakery display counters, and she proceeded to hang up her thermometers.

She covered the walls with these measuring devices made to look like the Eiffel Tower, the Washington monument, Monticello. Thermometers with silhouettes of cowboys and ballerinas and tugboats. She had shell thermometers and plastic cat thermometers, thermometers in the shape of bathroom scales or chalk pink flamingos who watched with one eye. She had thermometers with poems about this "Happy Day" and bank and coal company and automobile repair and grain elevator and diner thermometers. She had thermometers made of the bottom 8 inches of a deer's hoof, of coral reef, of lanyard material woven, of hobo wood etched in some train car on the tracks in Iowa. And there were story narratives to be read: thermometers with newborn babies looking into the eyes of young mothers, of puppies in a group trying to drink from a bowl and caught in the moment of spilling, families sitting down to meals of roast beef and browned potatoes and chocolate cake. There were brass hunting men on brass horses, the thermometer running down one of the horses's legs, a brass turkey from New England, a camel with a Bedouin rider, a round glass igloo thermometer with two Eskimos rubbing noses.

She applied them to the walls of the once tack and saddle, once Italian restaurant, once doughnut shop. She put an old desk in the middle of the room. She had a manual calculator that ran a tab. She faced the window and she waited. Inside the shop, she noticed, it was 73 degrees.

3.

We did not tell her about the man and his dog. We preferred to embrace whatever eccentricities she wanted to show us. We took in strays. We let them be, we said. All is good, we said.

In the heat of summer nights, we knew that out in the sagebrush of the desert west of town, aging burlesque dancers would have their annual international conference, dancing freely with feather fans, strutting gamefully on the planks of a wooden truck bed, lifting sagging arms to the stars. We knew, because he told us, that out on Fremont road a young man from Scandinavia kept his dead grandfather in a cave of ice, hoping that science would find a way to make him live again.

4.

At the grand opening of the Thermometer Store she served Ritz Crackers decorated with cheddar cheese pushed from a tube to spell out each person's name. People dropped by to chat and to see the heat of the day reach 100 degrees. Some of us stopped to see if any of the thermometers were wrong. We were filled with wonder that the red mercury line in the 350 thermometers on display seemed to have an intelligence beyond us. Everything in the shop measured. The white elephant with the ballerina riding it and with the word "Cleveland" etched on the bottom of its ear matched the polka-dot wiener dog thermometer from Minnesota. Everybody understood the order in the room and the joy in the good nature of the woman at the desk as she watched a 55 degree summer morning rise to a 90 degree afternoon in the shop that was not set up for air conditioning.

Someone asked her how many thermometers she had. She said 942, but that she knew of a man in Connecticut who had over 1500. She said she would like to visit him someday in order to see some of the instruments she had missed. Everyone agreed that no matter how much you strive to compete in life, there will always be someone in Connecticut ahead of you.

5.

When the movie theatre shut down because of leaks in the roof, we watched television on Saturday nights. We saw a program on television about artists. The narrator, a British man with a woven blue scarf around his neck said that Rembrandt was a collector. He said that Rembrandt went to junk shops in his town and brought back items that other people neglected. The narrator called Rembrandt "Mr. Clever Clogs" because the artist was Dutch and clever. We imagined that Rembrandt's house would have silver bowls turned black and woven shawls of orange yarn and yellow and white laces and black, wide-rimmed hats with feathers. Rembrandt must have loved the things as ornament. We could see that. Though as children we were told to set aside worldly things, we had to nod to the eye of a man who could, so the program showed us, make paint turn to satin doublet sleeves and who painted his own face, his self-portraits, over sixty times. We had to conclude that it takes a long time to see something, and even then, you may never get to its meaning.

6.

The town visited the thermometer shop for the sake of curiosity. The point was that we did not need five thermometers or even one. We could listen to the radio voices coming from a small town west of us. At 5 a.m., the announcer told us the weather and, except for occasional disasters of snow, he was an accurate man. We knew it would help her if we could buy one, but mostly we wanted to read the names of banks and auto repairs that had been thoughtful enough to give decorated, wall-hanging thermometers to customers as Christmas presents. We asked her how, should anyone volunteer to buy one, she could sell them. She said that one day she realized that these thermometers would outlive her. She had spent every extra penny she had, having worked in a grocery store most of her life, buying up thermometers. At first she had rules: the thermometer had to be in working condition, the name of the advertiser had to be clear, the telephone number had to be just 4 numerals to indicate an antiquated system. But in recent years, she said, all thermometers seemed noble to her.

Someone told her that when he was small he had opened a thermometer's glass tube. He had poured the mercury onto his hand and it rolled around there in a small ball like a shining planet.

She smiled at that fact. She said that thermometer behavior of that sort can be fatal.

7.

Mercury is a sprightly element. It is a poison. It is in the fillings of our teeth. She told us these things. Mercury can be used for medicinal purposes, or it was once used that way.

She said we should avoid tuna from certain seas. That the tuna absorb industrial mercuries through the skin. Someday, she mused, we should probably take out all of the fillings in our mouth. Someday, we'd know the worst of it. You cannot allow mercury to sit in your mouth for decades. Mercury is best placed on the wall in a glass tube that makes it appear to be red.

It was a snowy day. The thermometers all said 56 inside her shop when she told us the worst of it. She told us about a PBS program on Radium---another worrisome element. It was about a group of young women hired, she thought in New Jersey, to paint the radium faces on clocks. It was a factory in the 1920s. The girls sat at long tables and painted the dials with radium numbers. They used thin paint brushes and licked the points. They agreed the 2 and 3 and 6 and 8 were the hardest to paint. At lunch, because they couldn't resist, they went to the lavatory and painted radium on their own faces, green smiles and eyebrows and jewels in the middle of their foreheads. They turned off the light and laughed and laughed at the grotesque beauty the darkness brought. They painted their arms and legs, put radium earring splotches on their earlobes. Their hair glowed green.

Then they aged.

The radium seeped in and probed their bones.

It honeycombed the calcium and licked at the marrow.

They could not walk or even stand.

They died young, or if they lived, their arms and legs were broken twigs.

No one knew then, she told us, what radium could do.

But think of this, she told us, as we pulled on our coats, an emperor of China took a pill made of Mercury each day. He thought it meant eternal life. He had an underground tomb built, she said by way of closing, and made rivers of mercury flow underneath the ground. Imagine that, she stared out the window at the heavy snow filling the street. Quick and silver, she said. Metal waters.

8.

Tombs in China did not occur to us every day. We said she was a prophet. We considered buying thermometers. We gave away old clocks and Christmas ornaments that glowed green. At night we worried at the yellow eyes of cats that prowled the alleys. We whispered to each other about the luminous.

It dawned on us that something had to measure, that we had to find some order in this life before the gods handed us the paintbrushes.

She told us to come and sit still in the shop. She said it was a cave of quiet, that if we surrendered to it, we could feel the mercury lift up the scales when the temperature rose. She said it would cause a ripple on our skin as if the universe itself had made contact. We sat in chairs in a line facing the street. We closed our eyes. We listened to her instructions and we waited.

9.

Towns make monuments for moments that define them. We had a few in the park. Memorials to World War mostly with a list of the war dead. One statue of a boxer who grew up in a small house around the corner from the plaza, a banty man who appeared on television and who died in some unknown way in Chicago. We always said that years from now these memorials will be what is left of us. Look at the pyramids, someone said. Or the Wall of China, someone else added. And we thought of the Emperor floating in quicksilver.

The point is that memorials in our park inscribe our meaning, and we wanted to be more than war loss and pugilism. We wanted to point to our quiet knowings, our inspired breathings of spiritual essences.

She taught us all this. She started to give massages in her shop. She made yogurt drinks for us. She offered to put pins in our knees and buttocks and spinal cord. She made fragrant teas and had these Chinese cups that had ceramic lids and stayed warm all morning. We couldn't pass her store without seeing someone sitting on the small massage stool, his forehead pressed in a head rest, being massaged while someone else sat in the row of chairs, eyes closed and humming. Red faced and sweaty, she would be there focusing on her task, her doughy arms working someone's back.

Set inside the commercial frames of banks and grocery stores and filling stations, the glass staffs of red mercury on small bulbous bases were like thin flowers. They picked up the message of the universe and translated it to symbols we could read and check for accuracy even as we sipped tea from yellow Chinese cups.

We considered building an obelisk thermometer in the park, but to our dismay we found that the elm trees had contracted a disease that would kill them. The park would have to be dug up.

10.

In spring when all things shift, a glassblower moved in across the square, and we abandoned the thermometer shop. Through the window we could see the man at the back of the shop, holding the long tube and drawing the melting glass onto it, turning it, holding the molten matter in a wooden cup he dipped in water, shaping the form, giving it curves. We watched the man deny the lime and the sand their static nature. He melded them, that's how we said it, the word "meld" claiming our attention. He moved solid matter like taffy. He rounded it and pulled out stems for glassware. He made paper weights and pressed blue flowers into them where they writhed and twisted with their green stems.

We nodded to each other. Here is something elemental to us, we said. Here is a magic of fire.

We moved across the plaza. We watched.

We shifted, fickle of foot, letting the shopkeepers keep us vigilant. Sometimes we turned to ourselves and said, "We have all become 'Mr. Clever Clogs' wearing amulets of glass around our necks, going home to herbal gardens in pots hung from strings that we had braided, eating flax." It was our theory of thingness, we said, that saved us. Thanks to the thermometer lady who died of a stroke last year and who we found minutes after it happened, her bulbous face a bright red, we now saw that things have their own mind and our job is to discourse with them. That word "discourse" we learned from the used book man who moved into the thermometer shop when it went up for sale. He told us he boxed up the thermometers and sent them to a friend in Connecticut. Then he put in pine shelves and lined the walls with books. He showed us books on gardening and planets and raising goats. He had French history books and travel books about Tibet. He had old green books with golden spines. Some had engraved illustrations from the 1800s of what the world looked like to people then, of the things that they invested in, that river of metal water that encased them, the fashions and buildings and gas lamps, the way they lived like flowers stilled in a ball of glass.

11.

Last Thursday three of the old cottonwoods loosed themselves and fell on Rooms 28 and 29 and 30 at the town motel. They smashed the rooms and broke the beds and lamps and mirrors. Two of the rooms were vacant, and the third room had a single man who was packing his suitcase to leave just at the moment when the tree trunk caused the cave-in. The fireman dug him out. He is still in a coma at our hospital.

The town council studied the trees. They said that the trees were old and the roots were not getting water. Trees were competing with other trees and were dying from the inside so that we could not see it. One strong wind was enough to topple them.

No one said it, but we knew the kingdom of trees planted in 1929 was falling around our ears.

12.

Sometimes we wished that we had a talent. We said we should start collecting things. We knew how to do it. Sipping watermelon juice at the new juice shop in the morning, watching for a summer burlesque dancer to come in on the bus, we wondered why we never learned to do it earlier, what our contribution could be. Someone said that we lacked a vision, that we had no feeling for art-making. Someone else said that growing up in a town where a man was eaten by his dog did not give local folk a sense of growth and prosperity.

The Greyhound stopped at the corner. The driver threw candies to the children as he always did. Even he, one of us said, believes he is in an eternal parade.

We watched the tourist cars circling the town square. People got out, elderly couples on their way to Arizona, and walked their dogs, a silkie named Baxter, a dachshund called Nelson in a red quilted coat. We recommended restaurants to them. We sat on our benches, craning our necks to the sun.

One of us said that we were souls who did not collect things or make things because we just wanted to look at them. We let them grow up around us, hedge us in. We were not visionaries, not ambitious, not jealous or unhappy. We were not historians with accountant minds.

We decided to look at more things. Together, we walked to the bookstore to read the spines of books and on to the glassblower shop to watch the water sizzle as he dipped the molten glass and off to the corner where a young woman made "gourdens," gardens out of gourds. We perused the display windows of the soap-making lady who froze apricots into soap blocks, we knew not why. We passed the taffy shop, the Boots-Made-by-Hand store where the man drew your foot on paper and measured your ankles. And we walked to the center of town with the diseased elms.

There we sat down under the cover of the old bandstand. An old yellow dog was sleeping in the tree shade. We watched the dog. He was thin, his yellow hide stretched over his ribs. As he slept, we could see his skeleton move in and out. He was warming his bones in the sun. The bookstore man would call him an example of "metonymy."

We spoke the story of our town culture. That an ambitious man should have his throat cut, be decapitated for his greed, is one outcome we might expect. He might as well have believed that mercury pills mean immortality. We accepted that.

Then one of us said that when his head came off, a watcher watched. The dog saw it. And maybe the dog snarled or lunged or bit at the murderer. Maybe the dog whined for a minute and sensed the danger and tried to defend the dead man. But, we considered, a dog could not read the kingdom-thoughts of his owner. He did not understand the motives for marking territorial border lines of the cottonwoods or the reason trees fall on motel rooms. He only knew he was a chosen and, we thought, loyal companion of a crooked man who lived in darkness. We knew there was something to contemplate there, something to ponder.

We moved out of the shade of the bandstand and stretched out on the grass and closed our eyes.

We reasoned the temperature to be 95 degrees.

The yellow dog was still and asleep beside us.

We set our rib bones to its airy rhythm.

ON MERCURY

We could hear the snort and whiffle of its breathing.

We collected the sound.

The Articulated Fish

My articulated fish was not one of the six fish on the S.S. Medina in April 1917. But, then, mine is still an old fish, a brass and dusky fish. It has red eyes, small red jewels pronged into its head. I look at it and imagine the Sandy Point at Devon, the grainy beach, the pieces of seaweed blossoms floating, the broken crates from Calcutta pulled apart in water, the wooden slats and pieces, the chips of blue and white china cups floating, and red and yellow streams of silks adrift, the sea turtles coming up and watching with glass eyes, and, there, in the white water waves, the drowned fish, the brass Medina fish purchased by a Commodore's wife, the small and colonized fish, articulated, of brass, segmented, things that are a grammar of ornament. And, when that happens, I consider the poet who promised that, if we are drowned in water, in time, our eyes become pearls, and I consider the lady, her story on the documentary show, the crime show on tv, the lady called Pearl, whose husband drove a large rig, a market truck full of frozen fish, moving from New England to Indiana, and the story of this husband, Pearl's husband, who killed her and transported her body across the country in his fish van with the ice locker, and the rig became a frozen ocean, a room of white water moving in space, the fish and Pearl in transport, swimming, really, in air, in a Safeway vessel.

My fish is articulated. It has red eyes and a sort of smile on its catfish-like face. To articulate is "to join in sections" and it is to utter something, to express. To express is push out liquids and to utter words. So there it is. The connection between syllables and water, between eyes and words and pearls. That's what I thought about when the lady, who spoke in flights of sentences and waves of words, expressing, when she pointed to the "artic-ulated" fish on her sale table. It was a brass fish, a sort of catfish creature, like I said, a fish, about nine inches long. It had two side pectoral fins and a tailfin, called a caudal which, I do feel, is a beautiful sounding word. There is no dorsal fin on my fish, no pelvic fin, nothing to guide it or make it move, only the two thin pectorals hinged to its sides. It has a large and flat and naked head, two red jewel eyes framed in bent-brass pinchers to hold the jewels on the skull, as I said, and layers of segments, for the body leading back to the tail is made of thin rows of brass, layer upon layer of lace row segments, ornamental and moveable so that the fish can bend in your hands as you hold it, bend itself like a fish might do in water, so that, or so you might say, the fish can wiggle and struggle as fish do in the air as they leap or, as I say, struggle on the shore trying to live when, somehow, they find themselves out of the water. An articulated fish. That's how the wordy lady put it. The lady said, I have a wall of those at home in Arizona. She said. They're from India--early-1900s. She said, Medina fish. She named them for me. She articulated what they are.

Though mine is not one of the six historic Medina fish, it bends like they do. It is articulated, made of segmented brass layers. It has fins. Fins, you see, are distinctive anatomical features of any fish. They are boney spines. They are rays protruding from the body with skin covering them and joining them together. They are webbed things. Once a science teacher said, and I remember it, that the fins are not connected to the spine. They are for turning, for keeping a fish in place, upright, for stopping. He said frogfish use them for crawling and there are even fish, the reef stonefish, for example, who can use the dorsal fins at the top to inject venom and there is something called triggerfish who can squeeze into crevices in coral reef and use the spines in their fins to lock themselves in place. Fins are about place, is what I concluded. Fins bend the fish to the shape of water. You can go to Wikipedia and see this fish which, I must say, rather resembles the fish in the booth of the woman from Arizona. My fish.

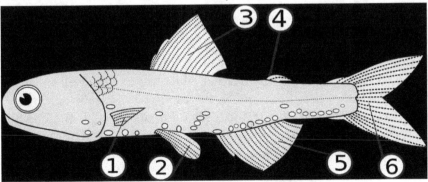

I must point out, though, that only Number 1, the pectoral fins, and Number 6, the caudal, apply to the fish from the lady from Arizona. Mine. Also, if you look closely, you will see that the fish in the picture is not an articulated, brass fish. It is a representation on paper. It is a drawing where the fish has dots for spines in the fins, and this drawing, you will notice, suggests the fish has a tossing of bubbles on its fish sides. These, too, are representation. Most of all, though, I like the way the artist put scales on the fish, on its neck behind its head, eleven scale-bumps, a suggestive bit I think, and I like the eye, a target eye, and, best of all, the long, and, shall we say, grin. While this drawing resembles the brass Medina fish, in part, it does not represent it really. It does not create the third space that my fish articulates for me.

Sometimes, I will admit, I find it hard to look at my articulated fish. When I was a child, my father fished. I would sit on the riverbank and throw stones in the river and watch them plop there. My father was an engineer, a metallurgical engineer. He knew stones. He built roads. He measured how much concrete and stone matter were necessary to make a road. He also fished. He wore waders, thick rubber pants with suspenders that went over his shoulders, leg boots. I would watch him cast his fishing line, mid-stream, and make it tease the water. I would watch the balletic fish leap and make a grab for what it thought was a regular fly. I would watch my father fight the fish, quasi-fling the fish to the river bank. I would watch the flop and flop. I would look at its yellow eye. I would look for pain. Then I would see my father slam the fish's head on a rock. I watched its body go still. He put it in a fishing basket that belonged, he told me once, to his father and I can still hear the backsong of the river, the slapping, slapping, slapping of the fish's head on the rocks my father knew. My father could name the rocks. He knew the names of rocks. Sometimes a word like "metamorphic" would be in my head when I heard the sound of the fish head hitting the stone.

I thought about knowing the names of stones when, the day I bought my articulated fish, the lady from Arizona said, "That one there." And she pointed at mine. Her small booth was full of Oriental art. She came every year from Arizona in her van with boxes of fragile, flowered Chinese bowls and carved plant stands. I knew her, her white hair and ethereal smile. Last year in her booth, I bought a wooden Buddha, a small rosewood carving, a sort of Chinese netsuke, hanging on a silk cord, orange. This Buddha hung on the silk like an ornament, a tassel on the bottom of his feet. Standing in the Arizona lady's booth, I played with the tassel. I had lifted up the cord, and I pulled the tassel and, to my surprise, the Buddha released another

Buddha, a small Buddha, an exact replica of the larger one, hidden away inside the other Buddha, a Buddha that begets another Buddha, a facsimile, a word I rather like, a copy, an inner self inside a larger self, a Buddha aswim in a second Buddha.

I should probably remind you that there were six fish on the S.S. Medina. Mine was not one of them. The six were called Medina Fish because, you see, there was a man called Carmichael or, some say, called Charrington, the Governor of Calcutta, a British man, who ruled the colonial island and, then, at the onset of the war, left Calcutta and his Governorship to go back to London. The colonial Governor and his wife, colonials always, packed up six full crates of things to take home, china and cloth and paintings, dark furniture and jewels and uniforms, embroideries and silks and six brass fish. The Governor sent the cargo crates ahead. He and Mrs. Carmichael or Charrington, depending on which article you read, would travel later, and that, it seems, was the issue. The six crates went on the ship called the Medina, S.S. Medina. There was a box of six brass fish with caudal fins and long smiles, in the collection. The ship moved through the waters from Calcutta, around the tip of Africa, and up along the coast of Europe, Spain and France, and neared the coast of England, Devon, Sandy Point. It was April, 1917, the war on, and there toward the South Port of Devon in England the Governor and Mrs. C. were waiting. And there, too, were the torpedo boats, German boats, that hit the ship with torpedoes and the crates of silk and china, or carvings and spices and draperies, went down to the sea. It sounds a paradox, I know, but, as I told you, the six Medina fish drowned.

Mine is not one of the six. It is a replica. It is an ornament. It is here on my table. Sometimes I glance over at it and see it is looking at me, smiling its smug smile. It is the only articulated fish I have ever owned and the only fish with red small jewels for eyes that I have seen. It is a representation that someone in India made long ago and someone else copied. It is a statement, you could say, of fishness. A statement. Like my Vietnamese friend who said that his family finds that, after a fish meal, the delicacy is the fish's eyes. It is good, then, he said, to eat the flesh and, at the end, to take the head, the skull with eyes, and work it in your mouth so as to suck the eyeballs out. He said it is a delicacy. He said I might not understand. It is cultural. I think of that sometimes. He said in Asia there are places where the chef carves a live fish at the table, section by section, and the fish squirms, struggles, and the chef covers it with a thin towel and holds it down with his free hand and slices it on the plates of the customers. It has a name, this live fish dish, but

I cannot remember it.

Sometimes I think how we are translators. I think of word-changers. I think about how we all do that—change words and play with sounds. We know we can make something horrible into something disagreeable, something apocalyptic into something merely in disarray. I know that. I know that the word "fish" is *poisson* in some places and *pesca* in others. I look at my articulated fish. He looks back. I have applied the syllables. Sometimes I sing to him, an old song, I remember my mother singing, "*Fwim, ted da mama fiddy, fwim if oo tan, And dey fwam and dey fwam wight ova da dam.*" The mother fish is teaching the small fish, commanding them, "*Fwim if oo tan*" and all I remember is that my mother said it was a song from long ago, from World War II, and I took that to heart. I saw how slippery things are. I saw *fin* and *swim* conflate, exchange. I saw syllables of sound. But what I really saw, if I am honest, is my fish *fwimming* for his life.

I have a friend who is a painter. He goes to pet stores and watches the fish in the aquarium. They know him. He's a regular. Sometimes he stops and they stop and he looks at them and they look back. And, anyway, one day my friend painted a canvas, a portrait, where if you look, you can see my friend's face looking at you from the other side of the aquarium. He is looking at you, yes, and he is also looking at the fish in the fish store tank who are there looking at him. You can recognize my friend's face and his glasses, and there in a square space which is the fish tank and the canvas, where time is still and he has painted a sort of self-portrait, just his face and, at the center, among the small fish, a large and orange fish with a yellow eye that is paused in its swimming, stopping, just there looking, at my friend's face. My friend is looking through the fish tank and he has placed the orange fish so that it crosses in front of his face at the exact moment that you, the viewer, see both of them. And, well, I remember that, the first time I saw it, I had to smile because, you see, this is the best part, the artist painted the portrait so that, as you look at it, you see that the man and the fish share the same eye. The fish eye overlaps and shares the man's eye and, as you think of it, shares your eye, and the picture joins the other two and your eye and the fish eye and the artist eye are connected there, all in water, all afloat, in slow time in a tank.

So, you see, my articulated fish, my fish made of brass, allows a third space for me, a space where there is music come from somewhere, where words change and there is conflation, where, for a moment, things live inside other things and wait.

Sometimes, and this is true, I pick up my brass fish, and I walk to the mirror.

I adjust the caudal because it is a good fin with a good word attached.

I lift the fish in my left hand so that it is level and we share an eye.

I hold it so that its red-jewel eye covers my blue eye.

Then I see myself and the other myself in the mirror.

It is quiet. Nothing is struggling.

We are a pearl forming in deep water.

ERIE

છ

What I tell Victoria who works at the desk beside me at the veterinary hospital is that we live in a space within a space. I tend the desk that checks in the dogs and puppies and Victoria checks in cats and birds. My desk has more patients so Victoria helps me, and she is the one who "Oooohs" and "Ahhhhhs" over the cocker spaniels and French bulldogs and afghan hounds. She is the one who talks baby talk to Billie-Jean, the Boston terrier who wears an Addidas hoodie. I will admit that I used to do that, talk to them like that, baby-talk to MacDuff, the Yorkie who leaps in the air and twists and leaps in the air again or Marcel Proust, the labradoodle who has the saddest eyes. I used to be like Victoria.

I sit at my desk in the waiting room area and look at the parking lot. I watch Muffy, the big and white-haired mutt who wears a jeweled collar, jump out of Rita's car and come toward me. If my check-in line gets too long, I ask them all to sit on the benches that line the room, a space where the wallpaper is filled with cartoon drawings of big and little dogs, brown and white and spotted dogs, all wearing red collars for accent. I check them in for puppy school on Fridays or for vaccinations or for appointments. It is a waiting room, as I said. Sometimes I watch patrons weep when a dog has been put down and Victoria brings out the small box containing the dog's ashes. Once a vet let me watch as he docked the tails of a litter of small yellow and motley puppies. I watch old men kneel down and kiss the forehead of old black dogs with greying muzzles as they say goodbye and leave the dog in boarding for the weekend. Truth to tell, we pay attention. We are mindful. The vet techs even write out reports when dogs are boarded. They watch and mark in comments on the dog's behavior: "Sam is a silly boy. He barks all day long at the other dogs. His stool is consistently soft."

ॐ

I am always at a waiting desk. Even at home. Yesterday in our local news-paper column, the one called "Giveaway" in the Classifieds, I read an entry that said, "FREE Fancy Guppies/Call any time after 11 a.m./Bring your own container." Someone said a guppy was any kind of newborn fish, any baby fish, but that is not true. I read once that a guppy is its own thing, discovered in 1859 in Colombia, and guppies can be flamboyant and fancy or plain. The plain ones are transparent, see- through, every vessel visible, like a toy fish, a clear lesson-for-science-class model fish. And I know that guppies are mindful, attentive. In every picture, the guppy eye watches you, its black eye intent.

I know, too, that Fancy Guppies, ones in the Classifieds, are high couture. Their tailfins are long dresses, the kind that you see in Latin Dance contest, the ones that flush out in rows and rows of material, layers and layers that float on air. And these are the male guppies. The tails flutter like a lady's opera fan as they move through the water propelled by their fins, their blue and misty, red and spotted, white and feathery tango outfits.

I know they search for things. They watch you as you watch them. One I saw was orange with a thin blue stipe. One I saw was yellow and green, a creature of water and drift. He knew his own beauty. There are films if you want to see them. In India, where there is a guppy farm in Kerala. I read that they film the guppies and put the swimming fish movements to music, a brisk drum, a dance, and they share it on YouTube. They even have a Guppy Trail Club that makes an album of the schools of fancy guppies, a float of blue, a collage of orange.

Once I saw a Fancy Guppy in a store. If you look closely, you can see that the male fancy guppy is smaller and more elegant than the female. The pet store owner told me that, in giving birth, the female does not lay eggs. She carries the babies inside her and it is a live birth. And, he said, it is true that, before birth, a baby guppy's eyes can be seen through the translucent belly of its pregnant mother. All is transparent. The Fancy Guppies swim and shift, wiggle themselves and look out of both sides of their face. They move their mouth-lips and propel. The female bodies swell and the smaller male eyes watch. The small babies wait and then come out into the world from the transparent case, moving to infinite space in a container in a liv-ingroom in a town somewhere, swimming among, swimming among, in a space within a space.

ॐ

I think about all of these things, and I try to see better. I am no longer like Victoria because in June, a friend of mine, Marie, died. She was the smartest girl I knew. We went to school together and she always was what I would call a source-woman. She pointed things out that I could not see. When I would tell her about MacDuff or Billie Jean or guppies, she would say that Nature is Nature, that to name it is to change it into a thing, to limit it. She would say that we humans make Nature into an object when we start naming. She told me that I must learn to see the stone and the flower and even Billie Jean as Nature pure, as non-thinking and mortal Beauty. When I told her about the parrot, Captain Kidd, who says, "Hello Baby" when the owner brings him in and "Goodbye, Dude" when they leave. Marie just rolled her eyes and said that birds pass by and that is what they should do. *Pass by, bird,* is what Marie said, and she added, *and teach me to pass by.* I think about that, the way Marie made a space within a space to instruct me that we are mere mortal creatures passing by, that we are things about to disappear.

Last Thursday a woman brought in a cardboard box. Inside was a woodpecker. She placed it on Victoria's desk and explained that the bird had been blown off-course by a gust of wind and had hit her living room plate-glass window and dropped to the porch. I told her that we are not licensed to treat wildlife, that you need a special license for that, a wildlife-rehabilitator license. I said the woodpecker was defined as wildlife. Then Victoria, my colleague, simply got up and ran to the back and came back with Dr. Ted, our main vet, who once studied wild things. Dr. Ted, wearing his green doctor scrubs, said he would glance at the woodpecker, its limp body now on Victoria's desk. Dr. Ted did not touch the bird. He only said the bird had either broken its wing or it was just dazed. So, we four all stood around the desk in the waiting room and watched.

The bird was motionless, its red-feathered head still, its black-eye inert. We waited. Then one wing stirred. The bird shivered. It shook. It stood. And Dr. Ted reached for it, wrapping his hands around its wings and body, and Victoria, on instinct, ran and opened the door, and then Dr. Ted moved out to the parking lot and over to the tree in the hospital office yard. He set the bird on a low branch. It tilted its head and looked down at him. It shook its body again and flew. Then Dr. Ted came back inside and went to help the black lab named Ledbetter, a non-wildlife specimen, who was recovering from surgery to remove three bladder stones.

❧

Yesterday, reading the Classified section of the paper, I noticed that the ad said that you have to bring your own container. When I called, the woman on the phone said, if you are careful, if you plant lots of plants in the tank, they will proliferate and fill the tank again and again. I told her I would think about it. I see these Fancy Guppies, come to us in tinsel drapes of red and black, of yellow and green, of blue with thin orange stripes, with black eyes and large red mouths. I see them propel themselves toward me, moving with feathers. I think they smile.

When I was young, when Marie and I were in school, I had seen a picture of a fancy guppy with its flaggy tail in a book. Truth to tell, when I saw the word again, "guppy" appearing after all these years in the Classifieds, I remembered the first guppy I had when I was small. The small fish lived in a small bowl, in a small fishbowl, in the small livingroom of our small house. Every single thing was small then. My parents were young. There were hollyhocks in our back yard. The house was white and small. I stood in the small livingroom. I watched the mother guppy, swollen and slow, swim round and round in the fishbowl. She was a patterned thing, the circling a repetition of mind. And, then, one morning, I watched as I had watched so many times, and I saw that the mother fish was dropping small bits of a new fish, letting go of her babies in the bowl. I watched as she dropped three and four and six and eight, pencil-dots, no more. The bowl was filling with sand bits that could swim, drop and swim, drop and swim, and the babies were swimming with her. I have no memory of the transparency, of seeing live babies inside the mother, so I was surprised that morning as I watched, but I recognized the circle swim, the lull of mind, the babies filling up the space.

I remember it was morning in the small livingroom in the small house. I remember there was the smell of grasses, wet dew. I watched the circling, the pattern, the contented blindness. These were not fancy guppies, only normal and middle-class and small ones, grey as I see it now. And, then, curiously, as I watched the mother fish, as I recall, no, I thought, it is not the mother, but, then, possibly, could it be the mother? I asked myself, as she would sweep in and swallow up the young. She swept and swallowed, swept and swallowed. I remember seeing my own sorrow. I remember calling out to someone to come see or to help as baby drop after baby drop was consumed.

Someone came. I do not remember who it was. Someone stood beside me. Someone watched, too, someone there with me. And someone's voice said, "They eat the babies." And somehow the fish bowl became another thing, a marble world, a transparency of ruin. They eat the babies, someone said again. You have to scoop them out or put in plants where the babies can hide or move the mother to another tank until the guppy babies, they're called "fry," are larger than the mother's mouth.

I stood and watched the mother guppy move and dip and feed and move away. I had no other tank. I had no way to save them. They were not larger than their mother's mouth, transparent as she was.

∞

I sit at my desk. I look at the parking lot. Nothing coming in yet. I think of Marie, of the way she always told me to think with my eyes, not my head. *Pass by bird, pass by.* The problem is, according to Marie, that we humans have to define and to make charts and measure and to name. The problem is that birds know to pass by and we earthlings think we need to make monuments to things we touch. The flower does not know it is a flower, Marie would say, and for a year or so before she died, Marie sent us all letters and told us that if we thought about trees and stones, we would stop seeing trees and stones and would see only our own thoughts and we would grow sad and remain in the dark. Marie said that she learned that, without thinking, she has the earth and she can know it, allowing it a passing. *Pass by bird, pass by.*

Last August, on a Friday, it was a rabbit. A young woman was at the door as we opened up. She was holding a clothes hamper, a wicker basket. In the parking lot behind the woman, I could see the long-haired white mutt-dog, Muffy, with her jeweled collar, coming toward the door on a leash for puppy play time. Muffy's owner Rita opened the door for the young woman. Then Muffy and Rita came in and waited on the bench near the cartoon wallpaper. The young woman put the hamper on my desk. She said it was a baby rabbit. She said she found it lying on her front porch. It was not moving. She asked if someone might help it. And, of course, Victoria hesitated and looked at me, and I had to say the speech about the wildlife license and I told the woman that there is a Wildlife Foundation in a city 60 miles north, in Erie, where they can help the bunny because there is a wildlife rehabilitator. I gave her the card with the address. She read it. She said, *Erie? That far? 60 miles?* I said, Yes. I said we had no license to help it, no wildlife certificate. Then I looked inside the box. I could see the small rabbit, its dark eyes, its long ears rising out of a dark-blue woolen blanket. It was a still thing, mute fur. And the young woman just looked at us and picked up the hamper and said in a sort of disbelief, *Erie? Really?* And she left.

I live in a space within a space. And today it is September outside the window, and I think about the woman and the rabbit as the leaves turn yellow and the snow comes overnight and is there in the morning untouched. I wonder if the woman drove to Erie and if the rabbit knew of death before death came. I think about the blue blanket in the hamper, the swaddling wrap, a kind of casket the young woman had made. I think about how she tried to stop what will be—the passing. Sometimes, there behind me on the waiting benches, I can hear Muffy's owner Rita talking baby-talk or the parrot on the owner's shoulder saying, *Hello Baby*, when it comes in the door, and I know the parrot does not know what *hello* or *baby* means, does not know it is a bird who is just passing. *Pass by bird, pass by and teach me to pass by*. I say this because last June I had a friend who died. Marie. She was the smartest girl I knew. She took her own life. I am sure she thought about it a long time even as she tried not to think. I remember her even though Marie always said that remembrance is a betrayal of Nature, better no thought, better the flight of the bird. *Pass by bird, pass by.*

BESIDE THE WHITE CHICKENS

1.

It happened beside the white chickens. It was a rhetoric of sticks and air and thread. The trees immobile and the water glass. The stick house and the boy who lived beyond his time. The boy who became an old man who lived in the yellow house and who would not speak of his life, but said that once, early in the morning, he, merely a boy then, saw the white birds of his farm, common chickens, lining the horizon, dividing the green earth from the blue sky, and there was a dewy and languid peace to them, this white stripe border, growing at the edge and shifting, moving the margins as the sun lifted, and the old man did not forget that, though he would not say what he had to remember.

He had never seen a tiger or a lion except in picture books, no beast stalky and thick, never seen a gypsy man sleeping in the colored coat. He knew no art but flat photographs in magazines he found in school, but he watched his mother once, his mother, a farm woman defeated by the cycles of the earth, as she did her stitching. He never cared about the things she made, the covers for the chairs, stitch, stitch, or the arabesques and flowers she put in frames and hung around the room, but, an old man now, a complaining man, a man of concord grape and dry birdbath, he considered how his mother worked the cloth, stitch, stitch, a red piece, as he saw it in his mind, with the woman in a gown and an animal, a sort of horse at her feet, and the tea flowers in the grass and the small gate. He never cared for woman things. He never cared for flights of fancy.

His mother sat at the window, stitch, stitch, her eyes intent on the piecing, and he sat at the table. His mother did not hum. He only saw her hand go down and up, up and down, a mechanical thing. She did not speak. He learned his muteness from her as he sat at the table, his hands flat on the oil cloth, waiting for some root-bound meanness he felt inside to dissolve itself, waiting to stop hating her and her creation of the flowered earth and the chalk horse, forming words in his mind he'd heard his father say, considering the young drifter who hung himself in the barn, his body swinging in the morning air, and planning how he would go away, leave them, leave the white chickens, that border edge, moving beyond to a space where he might not remember her, where common things like chickens were figments of a farm he denied because he knew that to revise is to move beyond, to deny the gravity of place.

2.

We schoolgirls all spoke of white birds the day they selected two of us to fly. All of us were wearing white—long sleeved lace dresses with high collars. All of us somehow knew we would not be selected, but all of us knew one of the two would be Arianne.

When Mr. Coey announced the names, Arianne and Sarah, as the two students to accompany him in a ride in his hot air balloon, over Chicago and into the countryside, we studied his fleshy face, his formal suit, the way his hair parted up the middle in an exact trail. We, the classmates of Arianne and Sarah, knew that Arianne would be selected because she had hair the color of a roan jumping horse and she wore lace dresses sewed by hired seamstresses who manipulated ribbons at her neck, and she never looked directly in our eyes, always over our shoulder. In her class picture, 1908, June, she had a beaded band across her brow, yellow beads with blue flowers, a band that fell in beaded loops over the sides of her head, and only Arianne would do that. She had a pearl bracelet and a gold ring, and she did not smile at the camera, she just looked pensive, distant, seeing through things like she always did. We loved her as we loved all tinsely things, all things that teased us into other worlds.

And we knew Sarah would go because she was so very smart. She knew science and physics, and she had been chosen to pronounce the valedictory address.

And we went to the park in August to watch Arianne and Sarah and Mr. Coey go up in the balloon he called "Chicago," the balloon that Mr. Coey told us was the biggest balloon in the world. And he ignited the gas and it swelled and there was the noise of the inferno. And we thought we saw Arianne wave at us, but it may have been Sarah, because they each became silhouettes against the sun. Later Arianne told us they floated over fields and farms that looked like little gardens laid off so well, and they saw haystacks that Arianne said looked like "clots" and the Page River that looked like a mere string.

And, Arianne said, Mr. Coey expected some difficulty in the landing so he gave them each a piece of sweet gum to chew and he told Sarah and Arianne to hold tight to his legs, and they did. But the landing was splendid, she said, and farmers came from the fields and helped Mr.Coey out and then Arianne and then Sarah. Arianne said they told her that eighteen automobiles followed the balloon, chasing it through Winfield, West Chicago, Batavia, Aurora and Sugar Grove. And when they landed, a photographer was there to take the picture.

Arianne said they slept in soft beds at a farm, with white chickens and a spotted horse, where the family fed them a meal of thick soup and soda bread. She said the trip was a great honor, that there never would be another treat in the world to equal this one.

It was months later that we thought to ask Sarah what she saw.

Sarah said she saw a fossil thing.

We asked if Arianne saw haystacks how Sarah could see Time in the stones.

She said it was metaphoric, metaphoric. She said it twice so that it stayed where it was.

We had to parse that, and even as we did, Sarah said at length:

Let's say you paint a picture and you change your mind.

Let's say you placed a cloud in the sky and a green hill with a few sheep.

Let's say you erase the hill with a grand smear of yellow.

And you replace the hills with a brown flat space, a desert, with drawing of a figure, thick arms and legs.

Let's say you erase the figure and put in a black and white dog.

Let's say you pick a word like "bird" and you write it on top of the paint that was the hill.

I say (said Sarah): You have added and subtracted. You have added by subtracting.

Then, (said Sarah), Let's say you are flung into space and you come back.

Let's say part of you never left.

Let's say you juxtapose the "self."

Let's say part of you, the part before the river turned to string, stayed here all of the time.

I say (said Sarah): What you are, then, is an image of pentimento.

And "pentimento" comes from "penitence" and sorrow and grief and sentiment.

See the rhetoric of sticks in that.

See, (said Sarah), the sticks caught there, the tall "ts" of penitence, the trees in the round world of smaller things?

They are traces of an ascent.

We did not know it then, but we would come to love Sarah as we loved all that escaped us like those yellow dandelions rooted in the ground that, come August, turned and floated on the wind.

3.

Upstairs in the house, he kept the objects. Small white bowls, white flower vases, oil cans made of tin. He kept them on a wooden table, together, close to two hundred objects. Ceramic boxes, shells, tall metal water pitchers with long handle stems that rise and pull off the body like a wing. He painted this, his second-floor studio room, a light grey color, hung rust-colored paper on the walls. He went there, up the stairs, each day to paint. He looked closely at three colored cups against the wall, at a fluted vase. He arranged the small sugar bowl against the brown box. He placed one large sea shell, the color of the walls and of old water, near the edge of the table. He channeled shadows. The room up the stairs was dusty, the tiled-floor old, the colors soft like sifted powder. Sometimes he brushed the paint on the canvas so that it was thin-layered and so that the brush allowed the morning light to filter through the design and arrive in a stroke. He allowed air into brushstrokes of the portrait of the small things. He abstracted. He muted.

On the floor below his three spinster sisters moved through the space, sometimes sitting and working embroidery or sometimes, in August, putting up sauces in jars on the kitchen shelf or sometimes standing at the window watching the trees.

He worked alone on the second floor. He never painted the sisters. At night, though, he considered the way the sisters moved back and forth and back and forth on the wooden floor. Then he would move to his studio window to look at the trees on the hills outside. Line in green. Line in green. Line in green. Blue-grey. He left his small town only once. He went to Switzerland.

For a time, he taught drawing. He liked negative space. For a time, he taught etching at the small college in the town. He taught them to see backwards as etching requires. He liked that, too, the seeing that halos things, the seeing around things. Well, he had wanted to be a priest. His sisters told him he was too crotchety. Better, they said, for him to paint boxes and bottles and oil tins, so he went upstairs and studied the quiet things. He painted three commanding white vessels, each ornamented with a rim or with a fringe of collar or with a sounded edge of fluting. At the back, but between them, he placed an old brown bowl, non-descript, plain and crochety. In the front, he positioned a peculiar rag, a cloth, at center stage, a workaday weaving, a household object, a cloth that requires one's hand to touch things. The next day he painted the same set of objects in the same order again, but not. This time the brown bowl which seemed to be in the act of disappearing in the first work, comes forward, defining itself, and even the brown rag is detailed with curves and folds of movement. This time, the white vessels, stalwart and feminine are thick with overwrought impasto strokes, filled with too much understanding, And here, in these two studies, the objects approach and greet you. They stop momentarily to prompt something, to promote some beingness, to become idea. They allow you time to see that, plainly, here and there, the rims and edges of all things move somewhere toward something else.

He lived with his sisters in the one house for fifty years, the four of them, virgins, spinsters, single things. They all moved through space of geography and sun, of grey house, of body flesh. They all looked for intersections. They all nodded to each other in passing. They were still, inner contained. They all laughed gently, covering their lips with their fingers. If they loved, they never spoke of it. There was no theoretical debate.

In one of the last of his paintings, he offers up a still life with four objects. He paints three clay cups, light grey, light rust, light brown, the wall behind grey, the table muted sand, the light source coming from the east. The clay cups share one shadow, and behind them is a pitcher with a wing of a handle. The pitcher is spare, monumental, but birdlike, the spout a beak. It wants to disappear. The cups, set in front, are a clan. Everything here is grey and beyond and mute. See this, they say as they start to move away. See how we know what to leave out.

CAVE SONG

The man who wrote a thick book said that he never named the characters because, as the man who wrote the thick book said, they are invisible things in his mind, they cannot be named. The man who wrote the thick book said, they exist there, in his mind, and he shares them, but they are not visible things, not to be named, that naming would impede them, that syllables tied to a thing limit the thing, code the thing, make it hard to in-dwell with the thing because the sound, the syllables of air, those sounds are instruments that shrink the object, that encourage quickened codes, that put things in an easy place, in a file in the mind, that make the invisible visible which, the man who wrote the big book said, it should not be because those invisible things should not be filed. He said the words he shapes, the man who wrote the thick book said this, the thick books are words that point, are traces of his mind and, he said, he stores them in images and we are, he asserted, this man who accomplished the big book, creatures determined by the images we collect, the way we see the old coin in the gravel or the cold green pear, the way the cloud over the hills is a grey swan and, look there, in his mind, he said, beside the cloud the black bird with the white beak, there, yes, beside the cloud swan in the sky, the bird who marshals the swans in the water by standing guard and shooing other birds away, well, that swan and that black bird, says the man who wrote the thick book, are invisible, you see, he translated the invisible and you believed him. The person now writing about the man who wrote the thick book and the concept of the invisible can see a white house in a town in southern Colorado. This person writing is translating by re-seeing a picture with a thick gold frame hung on a wall in a relative's house long ago, seeing this picture in a gold frame, a picture of a boat without a sail and some blue water. The person writing this sees in the person's mind that there is an old wooden cabinet with glass doors in the corner of the livingroom and it holds old and collected things, mostly glass things and, in particular, a ceramic piece, the likeness of three monkeys, a " Hear no Evil, See no Evil, Say no Evil" threesome. The person writing is old now but when the person writing was young, the person writing thought how strange the boat is, a sad boat, a tied-up-to-shore boat going nowhere. The person writing this had never seen an expanse of water, oh, a lake once, yes, but not a sea, not an ocean, not an orange grove, not a windmill. Then, from the corner, that same person writing this stops for a moment and hears the report, from the corner, on the television news, a report speaking of the twelve boys and a soccer coach in a cave in Thailand, trapped in a cave because the rain water, the monsoon sent water into the crevices, the tunnels.. The reporter is saying that one boy, one of the boys who has been in the dark cave for 10 days, said that he knew Time, counted it, knew the days passing, because he could hear the morning chickens clucking and the dogs barking. And the reporter said that maybe that was true, maybe he could hear through the half mile of mountain piled over him, but maybe he had been in the dark so long that his mind was making up the morning chickens and the dogs because, or so thought the person writing this paragraph upon hearing that report, there were no chickens or dogs, just invisible ones, because the inaudible sounds come through the air and we translate them, the inaudible and the invisible into sounds and images in our heads, that is, we translate the visible memory into images in our heads and we see the morning chickens and dogs because we need them, we need to do that. And the person writing this thought of the writer, the man who wrote the big book and never named his characters or the swan and the person writing this remembered that another writer who wrote another big book said that Time is a Room, and the person writing considered that Eternity could be Time or it could be a room or it could be a Place or it could be Pictures in our heads, images we collect and keep, a boat picture in a frame that was a dream space because all the person who is writing could see, when young, was not a boat world, not a water geography, but the dry prairie, the grass-lands of southern Colorado out the window, a dry prairie, a frame for the wind. The person writing this sees that the boys in the Thailand cave sit on rock. They probably have to drink cave water, flood water. They probably try to sleep. They talk. They probably cry. And in the severe dark, they only had images in their minds, traces of mind memory, store houses of pictures like a stamp collection, like the man who said his house, with the objects he collected, is a stamp collection of all the other houses he has lived in, and even in the house of the person writing this now is an object sitting on the side table, not far from where the person writing is writing, where the person can see it, and it is a clay object, an object brought from a place where there is a clay village, a pueblo, a clay statue from a clay town, a clay statue of storyteller woman, a clay statue of a woman in a turquoise blanket, wearing turquoise earrings, a turquoise necklace, a clay statue of a woman holding four clay children, all wrapped in her arms, swept together in her blanket as if in a woolen cave, and the clay children are holding their hands with long fingers up toward their mouths, their thin fingers reaching over their cheeks and toward their eyes, their wrists banded in white, and the clay woman holding them wrapped in the blanket with a turquoise rim and all five of the clay people, the woman in the blanket and the four children inside the blanket, all of them are singing, their heads thrown back, their eyes closed, their mouths open-wide in circles of song, their voices small instruments of throat and wind, and the clay woman with the turquoise earring and tur-quoise necklace, her arms holding the four clay children with long fingers and white armbands, this clay woman is seeing visions as she sings, her head leaning back and her eyes closed, and the clay children, their eyes closed, their mouths children-sized indentions, clay caves, child caves, singing and the statue sitting still, baked clay still, handmade, signed in Taos years ago, and the statue clay creatures, held in earth clay, five people, statues with their heads back and eyes closed and long fingers all reaching to frame the words, and all five clay people cannot stop singing, never want to stop sing-ing, cannot stop because they were formed to sing eternal songs, and the woman and the children, all seeing the invisible in their heads, translating soul-dream into syllable and soul-memory into syllable and culture-memory or blanket-memory or turquoise-memory into syllable, singing the invisible and translating it and listening, like the dark-haired boy, small boy, dark-haired boy, thin boy who, in the cave in Thailand, the dark cave where day is night and Time slow, the small Thai boy who says he does sleep sometimes, sleeps in the dark and allows the dark to talk, to sound of chickens and dogs, allows the dark to tell him that the visible world is a slippery place, that life is a gathered thing, that what we all must be collected, stored, that we can-not help but make the visible out of the invisible because we must translate darkness into image, that we are made to glean, that we are made to gather what we once saw, made to collect what will save us, a ragged brown dog or a clucking round of chickens or a clay woman, and we are made to listen for her, to listen to her somewhere singing, to notice her head lifted to the sky, her mouth a cave.

TWO OF ONE

1.

Anselme said the apple would decompose and turn brown and fall to mush and that we must contemplate the turning. He spoke to me, to anyone who listened, holding up apple after apple, reporting the Cameo and Baja, the Fiji and the Braeburn like prophecy, describing the taste of rivers and sweet tombs inside, the yellow stars against the red sky without. He knew cold words, defined the touch of dead men's skin, fantasized of butters. He tossed the apples in the air, suspended each in market light, in phosphorescence.

They decompose, he'd say, but rearrange. They guide the eye of birds.

∞

I knew what Anselme said required reckoning.

But for now, I preferred to stand in the back row. I like to be in black and white in a finished square.

From the back row, when they take the picture in black and white, I see the scrawny necks, the shoulder blades, traces but not eyes. In the back row my body will be missing when the picture, later, will be glued. Only my head sticking up with the other tall ones. And some teacher figure there on the stairs, dried out like a hunk of bread. Only the door with the screen and the white panels of frame in the frame of square. And beside me in the back row, a girl I don't remember except for the rippled wheat.

If you looked at the square, you might suspect the wheat girl is someone I know, you might suspect we talked, told stories, you might suspect you understand what you are seeing.

I do not think so.

The back row is syntax and desire.

In the back row you want to be erased because you know, if the one looking at the square does not, that erasure of the body is beginning, neck and shoulder blade is reckoning.

&

Anselme said the silk embroidery floss was blue. He said she intended to make an ocean, knowing that the silk pulled free only when the silkworm boiled away. She had dyed some threads in blue and some in green. She planned to keep her face down close to the work, threading and threading her way, until she heard cranes cry in tonal language, mounting thread on thread until a single pearl-colored wave commenced, her head down, lapping the threads until the birds complained that the sea was too vast, that their black wings could not carry them, thread after thread thickening in yellows now and blooms, petal after petal, tendrils, something clawing out against the black cold water, her spirit fingers threading dark night, all water space and petaling.

I can reckon this part because I wonder at the oversee.

&

My friend Selah says Anselme lives there in the ink, a haunted man, burdening himself with finding words. She says his hand, aligned upon our wrists, moves with the black ink in the old pen, making curls, his sleeve glancing a silver bowl, a dish of purple plums in pewter, a bowl or boat, as Selah says, for Anselme brings things from the sea, dragging gold gilt like samphire, framing cups he finds and suggesting the bowl was once for porridge or for soup. He said that, once, it moved with the sea, but now it must remember. I could feel the shiver in the ink line when he pressed down. And it will talk, he said.

Anselme seldom smiles.

I watch my hand write words. I see the rise of waves, the cartography of water.

&

It is a place of guinea pig cave and buried lizards and bleeding things. You bend your head. The overlap is there, the mounting up. Things marked present themselves in afterlife.

Some will say, Anselme told me, we are nothing without the mark. All is provenance and trace. The meaning is not the weight that keeps the soup from spilling, not in heaviness of silver. The meaning is the upbringing. It means by who that touched, by who that sat at table and spooned up the orange and floating carrot broth. It suggests, as Anselme knows, a gilded room with candles and servant men in black and white.. It suggests fans of peacock feathers. It is not perfect. It is spotted with ruin, holding nothing now. Its meaning is the then.

&

Someday, if I remember, I will show you the square in black and white. You will see me framed in the back row forever.

It will be in a book that I will put somewhere. It will hold some sanctity. It will be marked with a gilt-edge. In gilt-edge books there is always someone called Anselme.

&

Isabel is on the roof. I can hear her move, dragging that burlap bag she's filled with apples. I know she had dyed her hair bright red, the red of parrots, and she'll be on the roof for days judging what she sees.

I can hear her talking to the black birds in the tree behind her, the birds that make a croaking sound. They think Isabel is a wise woman. When she arrives, they descend into the cottonwood and watch her, their heads tilted to the ground surveying her hair.

I always feel a chill when she comes.

Isabel calls down to me. She tells me she speaks the truth. Isabel says she is honest and must say the truth.

I ask her what truth is.

She says it is what she knows it to be and she must tell.

I saw her for the first time when I was a child. The house is flat roofed. She had used a ladder to get there. Then her hair was yellow, the yellow of canaries.

I went to the yard to find something I had lost, a skate key, perhaps, or a beaded necklace on a string.

Isabel called to me, I am here now.

131

I looked up. She was sitting on a stool and she had a small table and a bowl of lemons. She was squeezing the lemons into her cup.

What are you doing on the roof?

It is my viewpoint, she said.

She had this kitchen device that kept the seeds out of the lemons. She cut them on the small table and squeezed them fresh into a yellow cup. She added no sugar, and when the cup was full, she drank it.

I felt my mouth dry as I watched her begin to chew on the rinds.

You were not born pretty, she said to me from the roof, chewing rind. And that will make a difference for your whole life.

∞

Isabel was there when my brother was born. She was dressed in blue, her hair peacock.

You must love him, she said, even though you may want to tear his head off.

I do not want to tear his head off, I said.

Yes, you do.

∞

Sometimes when the snow would come in drifts, my heart would beat with rare glad hope. I watched the front garden fill with mounds of snow. I listened to the radio, hoping that the snow would never stop, that it would fill the yard up over the windowsills. I yearned for the stillness.

I waited inside, never wanting to go out. I squinted to see the tracks of birds. I did not want to see the single and parallel lines left by a ladder, pulled by a woman with green hair come from down the street and through the gate.

She would be there, at the table on the roof, opening a pomegranate and sucking on the seeds.

I would pull my knitted cap over my ears. I would muffle myself in woolen scarves. I would draw the collar of my coat up to my chin, put on the thickest boots, and walk out, not looking back.

Hello, there, she would sing out. Hello. I see that you have no fashion sense.

She was sifting through the wet red seeds.

I see that there is no art in you, she said tilting her head, looking down through her green hair. I see you will thicken all of your life.

That is your truth, I mumbled back.

No, she would call, her cheeks filled with pomegranate, it is yours.

ଚ୍ଚ

Sometimes I sit on the sofa of my house and look at photographs. I can see my mother, fresh from the garden, her hair pulled back in a bandana, wiping her brow. I took that picture. I can see my father come home from work, his engineering pencils weighing down his pocket. There he is in black and white as I framed him. And my brother with the old collie dog. And my little sister with her cowboy hat, her red and white cowgirl outfit.

I have pictures of the trips to the ocean, of the fishing boats. I took the pictures of the group as we crossed the continental divide.

I have pictures of the blue mountains just over the crest of the hill and mountain cabins in the high country.

I photographed my father's coffin, then my mother's and the flowers friends sent.

I have photographs of buildings in New York and in Minnesota and in southern California as I learned to see ideas in stone.

I have photographs of the *Mona Lisa* and the *Mermaid* in Denmark, photographs of the Chinese warrior statues in the cave and of sacred elephants in India on parade, all painted in bright colors. I keep them in a book of culture and myth.

I have a photograph I took of a tree in Mexico with orange leaves only they are not leaves, they are monarch butterflies.

I no longer take photographs of people.

&

Isabel says that everything must measure.

Once, in college, she was there on the roof of my dorm. I glanced up on the way to my chemistry final.

She was knitting something, a long purple streamer of cloth. It matched her hair.

You know, she said to me, when you were little and learning to play the piano, your father could hear the money he was spending being lost due to your lack of a musical ear. He wanted just to put the lid of the piano over the keys and say, Enough.

I looked forward, continued walking to the Chemistry Department.

You have no ear, she said.

I opened the chemistry book. I could see the chart with the elements, the world defined by chemical weight and symbol. I chanted the patterns I had memorized to get through the test.

There is the truth of science. The elements combine and balance. Things move and change in the petri dish, a cloud comes into the tube. Elements deconstruct. Bacteria grows and we understand. There is a security in knowing truth.

I have lived my life knowing that to grasp is to find pain.

ℬ

It was in the heat of summer when I looked up and Isabel was there eating walnuts, breaking them with a small metal nutcracker in the shape of a brown squirrel. She put the nut in the squirrel's mouth and pressed down on the tail. She removed the meat and chewed, brushing the bits of broken shell on the roof.

Where did you learn truth, per se? I asked that day.

Long ago, she said. From sentences that chimed in me.

She continued to break nuts. Her hair was orange. Pancake-sized maple leaves fell behind her where the ravens watched.

And today, Isabel? I asked. What is the truth of the day?

No one will love you, she said, riffling through the bowl of nut shells, looking for one to crack.

It surprises me that she has come to the roof with her red parrot self.

I saw her last years ago, and then I taught myself to stay indoors or to leave by the backdoor.

By that time, I had learned her truth. I thickened. I lived alone. My shoes are old and worn and my white hair, when I pull it back, escapes any barrette, reaching out in all directions toward the sun.

I can hear her ruffling through the apple bag. I know she will slice one, cut out the seeds, and eat.

I sit inside. I imagine what this would look like in a photograph. A small white house with brown shutters. A walkway. A geranium on the porch. A parrot woman on the roof with her crows.

ℬ

Sometimes I walk past the town book shop, the shelves lined with books with gilt titles. I see the old woman inside, sitting behind the desk, reading, patting her hair. I know that she rarely has a customer, but she is there, reading. Sometimes a cat prowls over the desk, or a dog sleeps in the window. I see the piles and the piles of books unshelved as yet, a disarray of knowing.

I see nothing measured. I see a still world waiting in suspension like a caught breath.

I see the spines of books fading in the sun. I see books with words that no one will read. I see books that no one will remember.

The woman inside the window pats her cheek. That is all.

The dog wanders in dream. The light fades.

And the stillness is profound as it moves in the shop and erases names from shelves and the gilt-edged titles from book spines and lifts the woman and the dog to nowhere that I have been.

§

Sometimes in my mind I frame myself in my front window as if in a photograph. I know if I focused the lens correctly, you might see me as you stood outside. But if I could see myself as the photograph came to be, that is, if I saw my figure appear at the window, coming into view, so to speak, or realizing itself, in the developing fluid, I would act to remove me, my hand on the curtain, my face looking. I would defocus the frame, the window space. I would make it empty like a bowl is empty.

It is best, I believe, not to be the observed of all observers. It is best to keep everything at an arm's distance. It is best to erase the self as we, too old for lantern light, move to nowhere we have been.

And sometimes I contemplate the turning.

I take up the blue silk, the floss.

I thread. I thread. I thread.

I listen for the counsel of the sea birds.

CORRESPONDENCES

Something arrives, an idea, an image, and you are not what you were. For a time. Until the bones begin to stiffen and make sound. Shadows are surfaces and surfaces pass through surfaces and numb the glare like foliage emptied of description.

There is, though, that which I look at, again and again, the picture of Father as a boy, with his older brother and their father, standing on the river, in the middle of the river in winter, because my Aunt told me that my Father told her once of life beyond the frozen floor, where fish live there and breathe and sing and do not drown, and that, if you listen, or so she said of surfaces, you will hear them in the purling.

There are, you see, figures in a row in black rough woolen coats and ferns and river reeds like quick black lines, still and shadows of a bridge and someone else, a contour, not a detail, a surface thing of ice that connects the things about to disappear, a shadow of extension, a shadow figure framing without being what is dust become paper and all frozen, all cold, all frozen, reflecting, creatures with feelers and tassels, hoping for a translator to make them, so ordinary, into tinselly strings and words that want to say it, to speak the absence that makes the figures possible, the river and the reeds, black lines and possible.

I am writing to expose and to account, writing round and doughy penciled script, and sometimes the pictures and sometimes separate letters in cages and sometimes words that faster than I know the deer or the flower in my mind can read or know it when words that come are not words that were read to me, not words from picture books, but caged words come fast and I hear them and I scribble them in shards, in broken china pieces in blue and white, and the words are smart, sharp, peculiar, fast and edged, smarter than me.

ᛥ

I know you think I have forgotten you, but I haven't. I think my plant is pretty and it was so nice of you to think of me. It looks like it was trying to die but I do not want it to because I am going to take it home.

Emma White is here now.

ᛥ

I am sending this picture card because we are curiously interfaced, share a boundary, a fragmentary piece, I am , when I walk to town, and a deer is always watching, a mule deer with long ears like wings, a deer that wanders the streets and stops by the river.

I look each morning to see if my fingernails are turning blue.

Emma White is looking older I must say. She was away so long.

I can remember from years ago the way her black hair was a radiant blue-black in the sun.

☙

A book I know has pictures of France, a book for travelers, pictures of a place with wide aisles and spaces and mirrored walls of gilt frame and reflections and no boundaries.

The mirrors pick up the garden and sends it back outside.

I have planted flowers in red and white and blue near the house.

I walk slowly now on even floors.

I plant summer flowers and walk slowly and I know the deer eats colors.

I do not look in mirrors any more.

I see the deer watching. I know it is there. I am sure there are rabbits somewhere.

I know there are correspondences.

Not letters. I don't mean letters.

There are mirrors.

I am often conscious, but the sun is hot now and snow will come.

I almost combine. But I am not she.

I take the treacle syrup.

I sit at the window. I watch the yellow leaves fall.

In the morning the deer are there, in the yard, in color.

I see the orange pumpkins with welts on their skin.

I hear the train at the station.

Emma said once that the man at the station café is making ham sandwiches dipped in egg and fried.

He offers grape jelly, Emma says. He tells her to dip the sandwich there, in jelly.

It turns everything to Easter.

Emma said.

The sheets are stiff.

My hand is palsied.

Sometimes I close my eyes on Monday and it is Wednesday.

Will you bring a plant that does not want to die?

Long ago, you will see, I am standing in a garden.

It is an image of an image of an image.

I correspond.

I am not that person.

∞

A woman here painted the river by looking out the window.

Then I photographed her painting with a camera made of box.

The photograph of the painting of the river looks like a real river become flat in brown and blue in paint and then in black and white in chemical paper and then in my eye.

In black and white the river is in remove.

I enter the river. I feel the snow and the brush of lines, the branches in my hair. I make my way up the hill. I stop. I see trees. I notice they are pigment trees, yellow arms. I see the white Chinese birds. I notice they are made of thread, silk threads, white threads and yellow.

I walk on. I close the window. I cannot hear the river. In bed, the window closed, I cannot see or hear it coming up in rushes.

I know the story is contained in ruin.

The river is a black line, she found herself writing, no, no, I find myself writing.

Acknowledgements

"Erie," in the lines "Pass by bird," borrows from a poem by Fernando Pessoa.

"The Grammar of Ornament" cites a song lyric, lines from "Rocket Man" by Tom Rapp of Pearls Before Swine.

The last line of "Indexical" references a line by Jamaica Kincaid. The last lines of "The Tick Queen" and "Provenance" are from Shakespeare.

"Rhino" was published in *The Manzano Mountain Review*, Issue 2, 2018. The story was nominated for a Pushcart Prize.

"Even the Stones" was published in the story anthology, *Open Windows 2*, Ghost Road Press, 2006. The anthology of short stories by various writers won the Colorado Book Award 2007.

"Goose Summer" was published in *Open Windows 3*, Ghost Road Press, 2007. The story won 3rd place in the Ghost Road National Writing Contest. The goose summer/gossamer etymological link was suggested to me in writings done by the poet, Bin Ramke

"Provenance" was published in *Please Stay on the Trail*, Black Ocean Press Chicago, 2006.

The drawing in "The Articulated Fish" is from an article on "Fins" in *Wikipedia*.

Two stories were selected to be part of Reader's Theatre Performances. "Afterlife" was presented in "Stories on a Sunday Afternoon Stage" by Chalk Horse Theatre of Salida, Colorado, in November 2016. "The Tick Queen" was part of a performance by Buntport Theatre of Denver, Colorado, in a "Stories on Stage" presentation in March 2015.

I especially want to thank James Mitchell and Gene Hayworth for their love of literary arts and their kindness to me. I thank Aristotle Johns and Louise Olsen-Marquez and Margaret Whitt for their poetry and generosity of soul. I thank Brian Kiteley for his words, "Carol, now, mess it up, mess it up" and Gerald Chapman for his lasting and moving interpretations of literature. I thank Michelle Latiolais and Joanna Ruocco and Doug Asper for their always philosophical and poetic vision. I thank my family: David Reese and Lorraine Reese and Judith Reese and Erin Kelly and Carrie Kelly and Paul Spenst and, with special gratitude, Helen Christine Spenst who introduced me to Card Ladies. And, most of all, I thank John. This book is for John who told me the sky is blue and the sun warm.

CPSIA information can be obtained
at www.ICGtesting.com
Printed in the USA
FSHW021642270221
78997FS